THE
BIG TEST

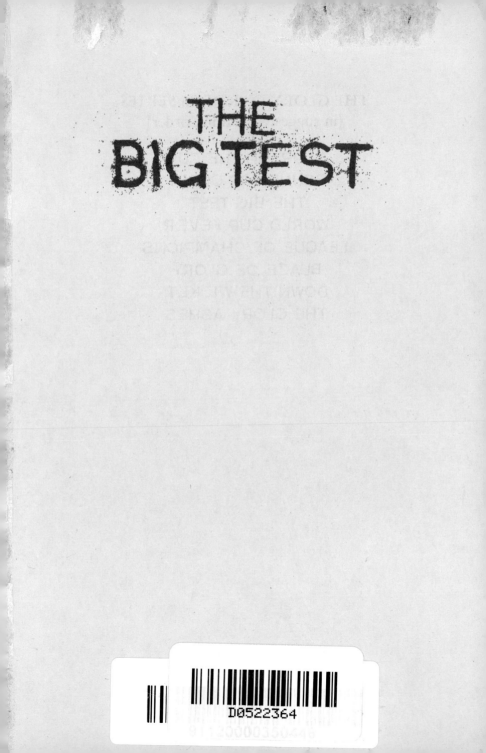

THE GLORY GARDENS SERIES
(in suggested reading order)

GLORY IN THE CUP
BOUND FOR GLORY
THE BIG TEST
WORLD CUP FEVER
LEAGUE OF CHAMPIONS
BLAZE OF GLORY
DOWN THE WICKET
THE GLORY ASHES

THE BIG TEST

BOB CATTELL

Illustrations by

David Kearney

RED FOX

A RED FOX BOOK 978 0 099 46131 9

First published in Great Britain by Julia MacRae and Red Fox,
imprints of Random House Children's Publishers UK

Julia MacRae edition published 1995
Red Fox edition published 1995
Reissued 2001, 2007

19

Set in Sabon

Red Fox Books are published by Random House Children's Publishers UK,
61–63 Uxbridge Road, London W5 5SA,
a division of The Random House Group Ltd

Addresses for companies within The Random House Group Limited
can be found at: www.randomhouse.co.uk/offices.htm

THE RANDOM HOUSE GROUP Limited Reg. No. 954009

www.**randomhousechildrens**.co.uk

A CIP catalogue record for this book is available from the British Library.

Penguin Random House is committed to a sustainable future for
our bus‌̲   ̲ from

Print‌   lc

Contents

Chapter One   7
Chapter Two   14
Chapter Three   23
Chapter Four   30
Chapter Five   37
Chapter Six   44
Chapter Seven   52
Chapter Eight   59
Chapter Nine   68
Chapter Ten   80
Chapter Eleven   89
Chapter Twelve   95
Chapter Thirteen   103
Chapter Fourteen   112
Chapter Fifteen   119
Chapter Sixteen   129
Cricket Commentary   141

Chapter One

"This is it," said Frankie. "No one's going to stop us this year."

"Oh yes? So what about Wyckham and Old Courtiers?" said Marty. Marty is the team's pessimist but, for once, he had a point. Looking at the fixture list it was hard to see a single easy match. If Glory Gardens was going to finish the season as champions of the Under 13s League we'd have to be brilliant in every game.

COUNTY UNDER 13s FIXTURES

Week 1   Glory Gardens v Stoneyheath & Stockton
Wyckham Wanderers v Old Courtiers
Waterville v Arctics
Brass Castle v Croyland Crusaders

Week 2   Arctics v Wyckham Wanderers
Waterville v Glory Gardens
Old Courtiers v Croyland Crusaders
Stoneyheath & Stockton v Brass Castle

Week 3   Old Courtiers v Brass Castle
Croyland Crusaders v Wyckham Wanderers
Arctics v Glory Gardens
Waterville v Stoneyheath & Stockton

Week 4	Wyckham Wanderers v Waterville
	Brass Castle v Arctics
	Stoneyheath & Stockton v Croyland Crusaders
	Glory Gardens v Old Courtiers

Week 5	Croyland Crusaders v Waterville
	Glory Gardens v Brass Castle
	Wyckham Wanderers v Stoneyheath & Stockton
	Arctics v Old Courtiers

Week 6	Waterville v Old Courtiers
	Stoneyheath & Stockton v Arctics
	Croyland Crusaders v Glory Gardens
	Brass Castle v Wyckham Wanderers

Week 7	Glory Gardens v Wyckham Wanderers
	Old Courtiers v Stoneyheath & Stockton
	Brass Castle v Waterville
	Arctics v Croyland Crusaders

"Oh but, what a lot of games," said Ohbert who'd suddenly noticed what everyone was looking at and was peering over Azzie's shoulder.

"I shouldn't worry, Ohbert, you won't be playing in many of them," said Marty cruelly.

"Course he will. We always win when Ohbert plays," said Frankie. "You'd be the first choice in my team, Ohbert." Ohbert grinned his stupid grin and then his eyes glazed over as he went back to listening to his Walkman.

Ohbert's not everyone's idea of a cricketer – in fact, he's not *anyone's* idea of a cricketer – but he was in the first Glory Gardens team and, for some reason, he's been with us ever since. Sometimes he even takes a catch or scores a run but, like everything else he does, it's probably by mistake.

The fixture list is twice as tough this year because the North County and East County Leagues have been combined.

8

Croyland Crusaders won the East League last season, so they have to be one of the favourites – along with our arch enemies, Wyckham Wanderers, Old Courtiers and us.

We're Glory Gardens Cricket Club – Frankie calls us 'the fastest improving team in the world'. Frankie's always saying things like that but even Marty would have to admit there's a bit of truth in it. Two years ago we hadn't even dreamt of playing together as a team and look at us now – we're almost professional looking . . . apart from Ohbert.

Cal, Marty, Tylan, Erica, Frankie, Azzie, Ohbert and I were all in the very first Glory Gardens team. I'm Hooker Knight, the captain and all-rounder; Marty's vice captain and he opens the bowling with Jacky, and our two best batsmen are Azzie and Clive. Cal, Erica and Mack are all-rounders like me. Frankie – he's the one in the back row holding the cardboard ears behind Ohbert's head – is our wicket-keeper. And Ohbert – as you know – is the worst player in the team and probably the worst in the history of cricket.

Back Row: Frankie, Marty, Tylan, Cal, Clive, Matthew and Mack
Front Row: Ohbert, Jo, Erica, Hooker, Jacky and Azzie.

Next to Ohbert, with 'Gatting', our mascot, on her knee, is Jo. Jo doesn't play for Glory Gardens, but she is one of the most important people in the club. She's our scorer and secretary which means she organises everything. Without her, Glory Gardens would probably just fall apart. Of course, Frankie wouldn't agree with that, but then he's Jo's brother and they never agree. Except perhaps about one thing . . .

"You'd better all start believing that Glory Gardens is the best team in the League," said Jo.

"Best in the Universe!" said Frankie.

"And this year we're going to win everything, aren't we?"

"Everything in sight. Hardly worth the other teams showing up. Glory Gardens for the League!" Frankie began to chant, "Glory Gardens for the League . . ." but Jo looked sternly at him and he shut up.

"Well, if we're that good, we don't need to bother with practising," said Azzie.

"Great," said Clive who's funny about Nets even though he's just as mad about playing cricket as the rest of us. "Let's go home then."

"Get your pads on," I said. "I'll show you how much practice you need."

Net practice is always on Saturday mornings at the Eastgate Priory ground. We don't have many rules but one rule is that you must come to Nets each week. Kiddo comes along to coach us – he's the opening bat for the Priory First Team. Kiddo helped us start Glory Gardens in the first place. We should really be called 'Eastgate Priory Under 13s' but Jo insisted on 'Glory Gardens' and, as usual, no one argued. The name comes from the recreation ground at the back of my house where most of us started playing.

Kiddo's a brilliant cricketer – on the other hand he's also a teacher at our school. He's teaching us French this year but he knows a lot more about cricket than he does about French. His real name is Peter Johnstone – but he calls everyone at school 'kiddo', probably because his memory's giving up and he can't remember their real names.

"Come on, let the duck see the rabbit, kiddoes," said Kiddo – he often says incomprehensible things like that. He strode over to the wicket and took guard. "I'm going to show you the most important shot in cricket. What do you think it is?"

"Straight drive?" said Azzie.

"Forward defensive?" suggested Matthew.

"Must be the hook," said Frankie, swinging his bat wildly over his shoulder and just missing Ohbert's head.

We came up with every cricket shot we could think of and still Kiddo kept shaking his head.

"All right, we give up," said Cal.

"Well, it's this." And he played a little push shot on the leg side.

"Oh yeah, what's that called then?" asked Frankie sounding unimpressed.

"I call it my start-up shot," said Kiddo. "You see, most batsmen get out early in their innings playing attacking shots before they've got their eye in. But you don't want to play endless defensive shots either and let the bowler get on top."

"Not unless you're Matthew," said Frankie. Matt scowled – he gets teased a lot for being a boring batsman and a slow scorer but he hardly ever lets us down – a lot of our biggest scores have been built round a steady innings from Matthew.

"Look," continued Kiddo. "If you've got a reasonable technique, you should find it as easy as falling off a log to play. Wait for the bowler to pitch one up on your legs and . . . thank you very much, an easy single. And no risk."

He got us all practising the shot. Erica was best at it; her timing was perfect.

There aren't many girls playing Under 13s league cricket. In fact I don't know any in the sides we play against. I wouldn't mind a few more in my team if they were as good as Erica. She's not just a good bat – she's one of the best economy bowlers in the side, too. One or two of the opposition players sometimes sneer about us having a girl in the team – until they

11

see her play. The only Glory Gardens player to worry about it was Jason Padgett, but he soon grew out of it. Jason doesn't seem to be very interested in cricket these days. He spends all his time playing chess – it's a shame because he used to be quite good.

Erica plays a forcing shot off her legs. The ball is going fractionally down the leg side and she waits for it to come on to her bat and then turns the face to help it on its way. Keep your head over the ball and it won't go in the air.

After Nets the selection committee – Marty, Jo and I – got together and picked the team for our first League game. It didn't take long because we only had 12 to choose from and we just dropped Ohbert. Jo said we ought to pick him for the next game though, otherwise it wouldn't be fair. Marty laughed, but I sort of agreed with Jo. In a funny way Glory Gardens wouldn't be the same without Ohbert.

Of course, Ohbert didn't even notice when I pinned up the team on the notice board. He was off in 'Ohbert-land', listening to his Walkman in his own little world. When I told him he was twelfth man he didn't say a word. I wasn't completely sure he'd heard me but he did grin and nod his head. Sometimes you just have to agree with Frankie's theory that Ohbert was put on earth to prove that not everything has a purpose.

This was the team for Wednesday's game against Stoneyheath.

(in batting order)

Matthew Rose	Mack McCurdy
Cal Sebastien	Tylan Vellacott
Azzie Nazar	Frankie Allen
Clive da Costa	Jacky Gunn
Erica Davies	Marty Lear
Hooker Knight	Twelfth man: Ohbert Bennett

It was our strongest side and we definitely needed to be at our best. To win the League we needed a good start and Stoneyheath would be no pushover.

"Do you really think we can win it?" Cal asked me as we walked home together after Nets.

"Don't see why not. We beat Old Courtiers and Wyckham last year, didn't we?"

"Yes . . . and then we went and lost to all the rubbish teams."

"Well, there aren't any rubbish teams this year so we're bound to beat them all."

"You're beginning to sound like Frankie," said Cal with a grin. He ran off towards Glory Gardens Rec. "Come on, there's time to bowl a few overs at me before lunch."

Chapter Two

We started the game against Stoneyheath with only 10 players; Ohbert didn't arrive on the pitch until the end of the fourth over.

Why was Ohbert playing at all? Well just before the game Tylan had a bad asthma attack and Kiddo had to take him home. Ohbert was twelfth man but, of course, he'd forgotten his kit, and, by the time he'd been home to fetch it and changed, Marty and Jacky had bowled two overs each and Stoneyheath were 13 for none. Worst of all, I'd dropped a hard, low chance at gully off Jacky's bowling.

"Take your time, Ohbert. We've got all day," said Frankie as Ohbert wandered on to the pitch still wearing his Walkman.

"Oh but . . ." began Ohbert – that's how he usually begins, which is why we call him Ohbert.

"He must have grown over the winter," said Cal with a laugh. Either that or Ohbert's clothes had shrunk. His shirt and cricket trousers didn't meet in the middle and the trousers stopped half way between his knees and his ankles. They were stretched so tight in every direction it was difficult to see how he could breathe . . . or move. He looked as if he was about to burst.

"Come on Ohbert. You'd better field at short-leg," said Frankie.

"Or silly point," suggested Cal.

Ohbert opened and closed his mouth like a goldfish. "Oh

but, I couldn't find my new cricket things," he said.

I told him to take his Walkman off and go to third man – or, to be exact, I pointed to the place where I wanted him to stand because Ohbert doesn't know the difference between third-man and the man in the moon. And, at last, the game started again.

I decided to rest Marty so that he'd have two overs left at the end of the innings, and I came on myself at his end. All the League games we play are 20 overs a side and no one is allowed to bowl more than four overs – which means you need at least five bowlers. Losing Tylan was a big blow because he was our top wicket taker last year – he bowls leg spin and he turns the ball quite a lot. It still left me plenty of bowlers to choose from although Cal was the only spinner.

My second ball was driven hard back at me head high and I got both hands to it but it bounced straight out. I tried to hold on to the rebound but I just finished up sprawling on the ground with the ball bouncing away from me. The batsmen ran a single. I must have taken my eyes off it at the last moment. I couldn't believe it. Nor could Frankie.

"Two dropped catches *and* he loses the toss. Which side are you on, Hooker?"

He was joking as usual but I wasn't amused. To make things worse Frankie took a brilliant one-handed catch next over off Jacky's out-swinger.

"See that, Hooker? Now that's how you do it." Frankie threw the ball straight at me at gully and I dropped it. Everyone laughed.

I was trying really hard to concentrate on my bowling but I kept thinking I'd let the team down. How could I inspire them to win the game when I was the one dropping the catches?

"The opener's hitting everything on the leg side," said Cal. "Keep it outside the off-stump and we'll have him." It's good to have Cal to talk to – especially when things are going wrong. He usually comes up with some good advice.

"You'd better go in the gully then," I said.

"Yes – at least when you're bowling you can't field there as well."

"Give it a break."

Cal laughed. "You could bring Erica over into the covers."

"What about all the gaps on the leg side?" I said.

"Tempt him," said Cal. "If you're bowling outside off-stump, he'll have to swing across the line to hit to leg . . . and sooner or later he'll give a catch."

This was the field I set.

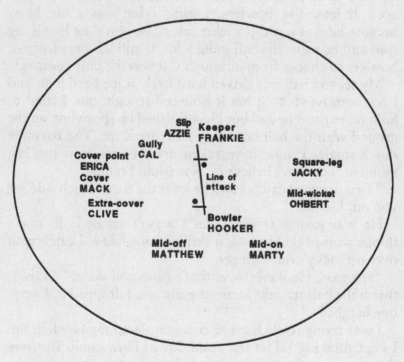

I tried to concentrate on getting my line right – just wide of the off-stump. At first, I was pathetic. I bowled a wide about three feet off the target. Then, trying to get straighter, I sent one down the leg side which the opener swung away for two over Ohbert's head. At last, with my sixth try, I bowled the ball I wanted: the out-swinger pitching on off-stump. It was just short of a length and the batsman swung at it as it left him and he got a nick. The ball flew waist high to Azzie at slip and he took it easily and threw it up in the air.

"I knew you'd get there in the end," said Cal.

We got another wicket in Jacky's last over. The batsman played a ball off his legs straight to Mack at mid-wicket and set off for a single. You don't mess about like that with Mack; he's the best fielder in the side and he was on the ball in a flash. "No!" came the shout from the non-striker's end, but it was too late. Mack's throw was flat and low and Frankie only had to take the ball over the stumps and remove the bails. It was out by miles.

Like most left-arm medium pace bowlers, I bowl over the wicket and my standard delivery cuts across the right-hand batsman. If you can get the ball to swing a bit towards the slips, you've got a good chance of a catch. For the left-arm bowler's out-swinger the seam should point towards first slip. As you deliver the ball, keep your fingers behind it with your wrist firmly locked. Push the ball towards first slip and follow through with your arm coming down your left side, instead of across your body.

17

That's the advantage of having Mack in the side. His fielding's always worth half a dozen runs and often a wicket or two. He's so quick to the ball and his enthusiasm rubs off on the rest of the team. If you watch him fielding in the covers you know that he expects every ball to come to him every time. He simply can't wait to pounce on it and hurl it in to the keeper. Mack's Australian. He's been in England for a year now and he started playing for us last season. Frankie calls him 'our best signing'.

With the score on 25 for three and two new batsmen at the crease still to get off the mark, we had a slight edge on them. I decided it was time to put the pressure on. I bowled a good maiden over and then I brought Marty back at Jacky's end with the same attacking field I'd set for him earlier.

Unfortunately he didn't bowl as well from the other end – sometimes fast bowlers lose their rhythm and direction a bit when they change ends – and nine runs came off the over.

So I began my last over. The first ball was a beautifully disguised slower delivery which completely fooled the batsman and he spooned an easy catch to Clive at extra-cover. The new batsman came in and immediately crashed a short ball back at me. It was high over my left shoulder and I dived and got my hand to it but I couldn't hold on. Again I ended up sprawled across the pitch watching Clive retrieving the ball as the batsmen ran a single.

"What do you call someone who drops three catches?" asked Frankie.

"Captain?" suggested Cal.

I couldn't believe it. No one ever drops a catch off their own bowling – and I'd dropped two. I walked slowly back to my mark. "This one's going to be fast," I said to myself. It was, but it was also a full toss and it went for four off a thick outside edge. The next went through Frankie's legs for byes. And then the fifth ball of the over nipped back between bat and pad and flattened the off-stump. I finished with three wickets for 11. Not bad . . . but I'd already dropped three catches, so that only made me even.

After 11 overs, Stoneyheath were 39 for five.

Marty's last over was almost as much of a mixture as mine. He gave away four wides and a no ball. Then he bowled a perfect yorker which was plumb lbw only the umpire didn't give it. It was their umpire – but probably it would have been just as bad with ours. Old Sid doesn't give many lbws either. At least it woke Marty up because he clean bowled the batsman with his next ball. He finished the over with another no ball followed by a nicked low chance to Frankie which he dropped. Marty put his head in his hands.

"Sorry, Mart," said Frankie.

"If you weren't so fat you'd be able to get down to the low ones," said Cal. Frankie pretended to look offended and rubbed his stomach.

I decided to bowl Cal and Erica next. I could have tried Clive or even Mack at Erica's end but she's steadier and more economical.

Cal may be the biggest player in the team but he's also the slowest bowler. He bowls off-spin, although he doesn't turn the ball nearly as much as Tylan's leggies. Batsmen always think he's easy to hit but he fools them with his flight and change of pace – which means most of his wickets come from catches. I spread the field and dropped Mack and Erica out on the leg side boundary.

Cal took a bit of a hammering in his first over but then Erica came on and bowled a maiden which tightened things up again.

"I want someone out at long-on," said Cal. "I'll try and tempt him to hit me over the top."

"Okay, I'll go," I said.

"No, I mean someone who can catch."

"Very funny, you wait till you drop one, Calvin Sebastien," I said as I walked back to the boundary.

Of course it happened. Cal gave the second ball of the over a bit more air and the batsman took the bait. He drove the

19

ball hard and high back over the bowler's head. It was coming straight for me. Then I suddenly realised to my horror that it wouldn't quite carry. I ran in hard. The ball was dying on me. I knew I had to dive. I flung myself forward and just got my fingers under the ball. Got it! But no – it bounced up and hit me on the nose and came to rest on the grass in front of me. What a nightmare! I jumped up, grabbed the ball furiously and hurled it in to Cal.

I felt a sharp pain in both my little fingers and my nose was really throbbing. But I got little sympathy from Glory Gardens.

Cal was standing with his hands on his hips staring at me. Frankie was lying on his back, screaming with laughter and kicking his legs in the air. Why does everyone think it's so funny when you make a mistake or two . . . or four even?

"How many's that, Hooker?" shouted Mack.

"He's lost count," yelled Frankie.

"Loads!" said Jacky. "Must be getting close to his century."

I turned and walked back to the boundary. But, of course, it didn't stop there. Two balls later Mack caught a screamer right on the rope and it all started again.

"Phew, I thought that was Hooker out there for a nasty moment," said Cal to Frankie – but loud enough for me to hear.

"Well caught, Mack," shouted Marty. "See that, Hooker? He uses his hands not his nose."

I tried to grin but it made my nose hurt even more. I was feeling really sick. Four dropped catches! I couldn't believe this was happening to me.

We finished off the tail fairly quickly. Erica got one, bowled off his pads and followed up with an lbw. Cal rounded off the innings with a beautifully looped off-break which just clipped the off-bail.

They were all out in the 19th over for 70. It could have been worse. But, without my help, it would have been a lot better, too. My throbbing fingers and nose just reminded me all the more how useless I'd been.

"Never mind, Hooknose," said Frankie. "You go and have a blow and wash the butter off your fingers."

"Leave it to us to win the game," said Cal, slapping me on the back.

Kiddo came over with Gatting waddling and panting after him. Gatting's almost as old as Kiddo. He's a nice old mongrel but these days he's getting a bit overweight and smelly. For some reason he's been adopted as our team mascot – represented by the squidgy black thing my sister made which is supposed to be modelled on Gatting, though it doesn't look a bit like him really.

"Are you all right, kiddo?" Kiddo took a close look at my nose and both my fingers and said that he didn't think anything was broken. "Mind you, if you're still in pain after the game, we'll go and get an X-ray. Perhaps you'd better not bat."

"I'm fine, honest," I said. There was no way I wasn't going to bat.

"Apart from wounded pride, eh?"

"Well, have you ever dropped four catches in a game?"

"Eh, not exactly, but I think I dropped three once. Sometimes all the difficult chances just follow you around."

"That first caught and bowled wasn't difficult."

"Forget it, kiddo. Worry about winning the game instead. It's only three and a half runs an over you need. Tell them not to go mad and you'll win easily."

21

HOME TEAM	GLORY GARDENS	V	STONEYHEATH K S	AWAY TEAM	AT	EASTGATE PRIORY
					DATE	MAY 4TH

INNINGS OF STONEYHEATH   **TOSS WON BY** HEATH   **WEATHER** SUNNY

BATSMAN	RUNS SCORED	HOW OUT	BOWLER	SCORE
10. SHERINGHAM	1.2.1.1.1.2 >>	ct NAZAR	KNIGHT	8
2 M. AYMES	1.2.1.1.2 >>	ct ALLEN	GUNN	7
3 R. RUSSELL	2 >>	ct DA COSTA	KNIGHT	2
4 T. SANDALL	>>	RUN	OUT	0
5 A. WADE	4.1.4 >>	bowled	KNIGHT	9
6 W. EKE	1	bowled	LEAR	1
7 J. DONOHUE	1.3.1.1.2 >>	bowled	DAVIES	8
8 B. FLAVELL	2.1 >>	ct McCURDY	SEBASTIEN	3
9 J. GUPTE	>>	lbw	DAVIES	0
10 T. BARR	1.2.1.(.1	NOT	OUT	6
11 B. LAMB	1.1. >>	bowled	SEBASTIEN	2

FALL OF WICKETS

	1	2	3	4	5	6	7	8	9	10
SCORE	18	21	25	33	38	45	56	60	67	70
BAT NO	2	1	4	3	5	6	8	7	9	10

BYES	1.1.2.1.1.2.2	11
L BYES	1.1.1	3
WIDES	1.1.1.4	7
NO BALLS	1.1.1	3

TOTAL EXTRAS	24
TOTAL FOR	70
WKTS	10

SCORE AT A GLANCE

BOWLING ANALYSIS ⊙ NO BALL + WIDE

BOWLER	1	2	3	4	5	6	7	8	9	10	11	12	13	OVS	MDS	RUNS	WKT
1 M. LEAR	.0.1 ...1	.1. ..1	X	.4. +.2.	.3.1 +.0	X								4	0	18	1
2 J. GUNN	.2. 1..	..2 ..1	2.W ...	.+. ..1	X									4	0	9	1
3 H. KNIGHT	.1. ..1	+.2 .W.	M	N14 .W1	X									4	1	11	3
4 C. SEBASTIEN	.3. 2.11	.1. .W.	..2 ..1	1.1 W										3.4	0	13	2
5 E. DAVIES	M	.2. .W1	..1 W.1											3	1	5	2
6																	
7																	
8																	
9																	

Chapter Three

I looked at Jo's scorecard on the way back to the changing room.

"Least it doesn't show dropped catches," I said.

"Oh, that's all right, Hooker," said Jo, "I keep a record of them in my little note book here. Four, wasn't it?" And she pushed the note book under my sore nose.

"The last one was impossible," I mumbled.

That wasn't what they thought in the changing room.

"Cal's theory is that you were trying to head that last one to Mack," began Frankie.

"But you nosed it instead," said Azzie.

"We ought to call him Hooter instead of Hooker," said Frankie peering closely at my red nose.

"Don't take any notice of them Hooker, mate," said Mack. "I think that red blob in the middle of your face really suits you."

I tried to ignore the jokes and look as if I didn't care. "Hurry up and get your pads on," I said to Cal and Matthew, and I walked out of the changing room to more hoots of laughter.

I was pretty miserable about the dropped catches but I still had to make sure that everyone was concentrating on winning the game.

"Keep it tight for the first couple of overs," I said to Cal and Matthew as they went out. "We're not in a hurry and we'll win if we don't lose early wickets."

"Leave it to us," said Matthew.

The Stoneyheath opening attack was steady. Neither of the bowlers was as quick as Marty, but they were quite accurate and Cal and Matthew both took a bit of time to settle in. For once Matthew outscored Cal, which is a sure sign that the runs aren't coming very quickly. Matthew's the most defensive player in the team – I don't think I can remember him ever playing across the line or hitting the ball in the air. Certainly not early in the innings anyway. If the ball's outside the off-stump he leaves it. If it's straight he's right forward or right back. He almost looks as if he's sniffing the ball when he plays it.

After six overs we'd crept to 13 for none and the run rate required had climbed to over four an over. Nothing to worry about yet but it would be nice to see a few more runs on the board.

Then both Cal and Matthew were out in quick succession. Cal went for a ball wide of the off-stump and was caught behind and Matthew left one which cut back and shaved his wicket, just enough to dislodge one bail.

So Azzie and Clive were at the wicket together. Everyone remembered the occasion last year when Azzie hit his great 50 and Clive had tried his best to stop him getting it by farming all the bowling. What would happen this time? You can never tell with Clive; he can be either a genius or a pain in the neck – and often he's both at the same time. Today he was on fire. From the very first ball he received – a graceful flick off his pads down to deep square-leg – you could tell he was completely in command. He was on 9 before Azzie even got off the mark and, although Azzie played well, for once he was outshadowed by Clive. To be fair, Clive got more of the strike but Azzie didn't mind that. If the team's scoring runs, he's happy.

Clive started to demolish the bowling. His best shot was a perfectly timed pull which whistled along the ground to the right of square-leg for four.

Clive plays the pull shot early like Brian Lara. First his weight goes on the back foot. He is chest on to the bowler when he hits the ball and he strikes it well in front of his body with his weight finishing on his front foot. As he follows through he watches the ball speeding to the boundary square of the wicket.

The runs came quickly and after twelve overs we were on 43. Then they brought on a spinner. Clive went down the wicket to him and hit him over the top. But when he tried the same tactic two balls later he missed and was stumped. He slapped his bat against his pad in annoyance and walked off to cheers and applause from the Glory Gardens bench. He'd scored 20 at well over a run a ball.

Both Erica and I were padded up and she got up to bat.

"I think I'll go in next," I said.

She looked at me. "But I always go in five . . ." she began.

"Just an experiment," I muttered and I set off for the wicket.

I don't know why I did it. Perhaps I felt I had something to prove after dropping all those catches. It was a spur-of-the-moment sort of thing. I didn't think about it, I just decided and that was it. But I knew as I walked to the wicket that Erica would be upset. I would have been in her place. I mean, you don't just change the batting order at the last minute without explaining things to people. She'd have been preparing herself for her innings and now she didn't know when she'd be in.

Azzie met me in the middle.

"Where's Erica? Not ill is she?"

"No. I just changed the order. Captains can do that, can't they?" I was cross with myself now and I was taking it out on Azzie.

"Okay, okay," he said, looking a bit surprised. "So let's get the runs."

I watched the spinner carefully – he was turning it a bit. At the other end Azzie was scoring freely. The best thing was to give him as much of the strike as I could. I got off the mark with an off-drive which took a thick inside edge to mid-wicket. That brought up the 50.

Azzie got a four with a cracking cover drive and then played on, pulling a shortish ball on to his stumps.

I watched Erica walk slowly out to the wicket. As she passed me she said, "I suppose it's my turn now. Or would you like someone else to go ahead of me?"

I started to say something but she just snapped, "Be ready to run," and strode off to take her guard.

She pushed her first ball down on the leg side and called for a single. I only just made it before the fielder hit the stumps with a direct throw. If I didn't know Erica better I would have sworn that she'd tried to run me out.

I kept the bowling with a single off the last ball of the over. And then I hit the spinner for a four and a two – both swept square. A bye gave me the strike again.

We now needed only five to win and I was facing a new bowler. He bowled a full toss and I clipped it off my legs for two. The next ball was another full toss and I cracked it past square-leg for four. And that was it. We'd won easily with six wickets and more than two overs to spare.

I caught up with Erica who was walking quickly back to the pavilion.

"A good win," I said feebly.

"And a good bat for me. I only faced one ball."

"And nearly ran me out."

"Should have tried harder then, shouldn't I?"

I've never seen Erica so angry. I thought I'd better let her cool down.

"Well, dropped catches win matches," said Cal to me with a grin. "Played one, won one."

Kiddo came into the changing room to congratulate us. "Well played, kiddoes. That was a good show."

"Glory Gardens – number one. Look out Waterville, here we come," chanted Frankie.

"You've still got a lot to improve on if you want to win the League," said Kiddo.

"Like Hooter's catching," said Frankie, giving me a nudge.

"And your wicket-keeping," said Jacky. "Do you know 'byes' was their top scorer with 11."

"That's right," said Kiddo. "We've got to tighten up on the fielding – and the wides and no balls, too. They got 24 extras and that's far too many in a score of 70."

Erica was talking to Jo when I came out of the changing room. She walked straight up to me.

"Look, Hooker, I won't go on about this, but I like to know what number I'm batting more than two seconds before I go in."

"Yes, I'm sorry. It was a mistake."

"I mean I don't mind batting five or six. I just like to know beforehand."

27

"I said, it was a mistake. I was wrong."

She looked at me coldly.

"You'll be five next week," I said.

"Okay . . . and, Hooker." She grinned. "Well batted."

"Thanks."

"Wait," Frankie came bursting out of the pavilion wearing a baseball cap with what looked like a small cricket bat stuck through his head. The handle was at the front and the blade went straight through the cap and stuck out at the back. "We haven't voted for the Man of the Match yet," he shouted.

"What Man of the Match?" asked Cal.

"It's my new idea," said Frankie. "All take a piece of paper and write down the name of your Man of the Match."

He handed out some scraps of paper which looked as though they'd been ripped out of his school maths book and we all wrote down our choice and handed them back to Frankie.

He started counting them; then he dropped them all and got in such a mess that Jo came over and took them away from him. "Give them to me," she said. "It'll take you all night."

She quickly added up the results and announced them. "Votes for *Player* of the Match," said Jo with a stern look at Frankie. I was beginning to feel a bit sorry for him – after all it was his idea. Jo read out her list:

Ohbert	1 vote
Gatting	1 vote
Hooker	2 votes
Clive	8 votes

Clive looked pleased until Frankie held up the baseball cap. "The Man, er Player of the Match has to wear this until the next game," and he plonked it on Clive's head.

"Who did you vote for, Clive?" asked Mack.

"Me, of course," said Clive.

"Then who voted for Ohbert?" asked Frankie.

28

HOME TEAM	GLORY GARDENS	V	STONEYHEATH K.S.	AWAY TEAM	AT	EASTGATE PRIORY

DATE MAY 4TH

INNINGS OF GLORY GARDENS .... TOSS WON BY S'HEATH WEATHER SUNNY.

BATSMAN	RUNS SCORED	HOW OUT	BOWLER	SCORE
1 M. ROSE	1·1·2·1	bowled	GUPTE	5
2 C. SEBASTIEN	1·1·1·2	ct SANDALL	RUSSELL	5
3 A. NAZAR	1·2·1·3·2·2·1·4	bowled	BARR	16
4 C. DA COSTA	2·1·2·2·1·1·1·4·1·2·1·2	st SANDALL	EKE	20
5 H. KNIGHT	2·1·1·4·2·2·4	NOT	OUT	16
6 E. DAVIES	1·	NOT	OUT	1
7				
8				
9				
10				
11				

FALL OF WICKETS

	1	2	3	4	5	6	7	8	9	10
SCORE	17	17	45	57						
BAT NO	2	1	4	3						

BYES	1·1·2·1	5
LEGBYES	1·1	2
WIDES		
NO BALLS	1·1	2

TOTAL EXTRAS 9
TOTAL FOR 72
WKTS 4

SCORE AT A GLANCE

BOWLING ANALYSIS ⊙ NO BALL + WIDE

BOWLER	1	2	3	4	5	6	7	8	9	10	11	12	13	OVS	MDS	RUNS	WKT
1 R. RUSSELL	:·:·/·1	·/·2··	::··	·2·/·W										4	0	7	1
2 J. GUPTE	1·:·	:·/··	⊙··	W·2··										4	0	7	1
3 B. FLAVELL	2·2·1··	·2·1··	4/·⊙2/											2	0	14	0
4 T. BARR	·1·1··	3·2·1··	2··2·1	·4W·1·1										4	0	19	1
5 W. EKE	·2·W··	·2·1·1	·4·2··											3	0	12	1
6 A. WADE	24													0-2	0	6	0
7																	
8																	
9																	

Chapter Four

Glory Gardens *beat* **Stoneyheath & Stockton by six wickets**
Wyckham Wanderers *beat* **Old Courtiers by two wickets**
Waterville *lost to* **Arctics by 22 runs**
Brass Castle *lost to* **Croyland Crusaders by 15 runs**

	Played	W	L	Pts
Arctics	1	1	0	10
Croyland	1	1	0	10
Glory Gardens	1	1	0	10
Wyckham	1	1	0	10
Brass Castle	1	0	1	0
Old Courtiers	1	0	1	0
Stoneyheath	1	0	1	0
Waterville	1	0	1	0

After Wednesday night's cricket, Saturday is usually the best day of the week. It starts with knowing that there's no school for two days and then on Saturday morning it's Nets at the Priory.

But this Saturday was different. It was the day when a lot of problems started for me and for Glory Gardens. It began well enough. The sun was shining and there were last week's scores up on the Eastgate Priory notice board.

"Oh but, I thought you said we'd be top," said Ohbert.

"We are, dumbo," said Marty. "We're equal top but they put them in alphabetical order. We're a G so we come after Arctics and Croyland."

"Shouldn't we change our name to begin with an A then?" said Ohbert.

"Like Aardvarks?" suggested Frankie. "Or Animals?"

I couldn't make up my mind whether I was pleased or not that Wyckham had beaten Old Courtiers. Wyckham were 'Enemy No. 1' – so we always wanted them to lose – but Old Courtiers were probably the best all-round team in the League, so it was good they'd dropped some points.

"Bighead Katz got 50," said Marty. Liam Katz was the captain of Wyckham Wanderers.

"Who told you?" asked Azzie.

"Bighead himself. He saw me yesterday and started waving at me. I knew that meant he had something to boast about. And guess what he said?"

"I got a brilliant 50!" said Cal and Azzie together.

"Word perfect," said Marty.

"Typical Katzy," said Frankie. "You know, his fanmail keeps him really busy; not reading it, writing it."

Kiddo arrived for net practice – and that's when things started going wrong.

"I've had a call from Waterville, kiddoes," he said. "They want to play the game next Saturday afternoon – is that okay with you lot?"

Everyone, including me, said, "Yes." Then I suddenly remembered, I wouldn't be there. *My family were going away for the weekend!* I'd moaned about it but my mum had said, "We can't stay at home every weekend just because you've net practice and it's ages since we've seen Uncle Pete and Aunt Eileen. You know you like seeing them." Yeah, in the winter, maybe. Missing Nets was one thing – missing a crucial game was disaster . . . Maybe I could persuade them to let me stay on my own. But I knew really there was no chance. When my mum makes her mind up she's as bad as my sister.

I told Cal the awful news.

"Never mind, perhaps you need a break to get over the last game," he said.

"Don't be an idiot, it's only the second game of the season."

"I mean your injuries."

One of my fingers was still sore and my nose had gone a bit black at the top – but there was no way it was going to stop me playing cricket.

"Perhaps I should run away."

"They'd know where to find you, wouldn't they? Just turn up at Waterville cricket ground."

After that terrible news I didn't really enjoy Nets. Everyone was there except Jacky who had a cold and Matthew who was on the Knicker Rota.

The Knicker Rota is how we make money for Glory Gardens. Tylan's dad has a stall in the Horsefair Market and he used to make Tylan work for him on Saturday mornings when it's really busy. That meant Tylan missed Nets every week until Erica had the idea that we could all take turns. It's worked out really well because we earn lots of money from people telling us to keep the change and it all goes into the Glory Gardens Giro Account. We've got £77.80 in it at the moment, so Matthew says; he's the Treasurer. We call it the 'Knicker Rota' because that's what Tylan's old man sells . . . knickers and underwear and stuff like that.

Kiddo split us into two groups. One lot practised close catching up against the wall by the pavilion.

The rest of us went into the nets and concentrated on playing balls outside the off-stump. Kiddo showed us which balls to leave alone and which ones to play.

"You've got to learn where your off-stump is, kiddoes," he kept saying.

"It's the one on the left," whispered Frankie to Ohbert.

As usual Kiddo droned on with us only half listening. He likes to use important sounding expressions about 'bowlers bowling down the corridor of uncertainty' and 'keeping the batsman in two minds' but I think it all came down to two things: early in your innings leave the ball outside the off-stump unless it's pitched-up to drive; and, when you drive, get your front foot across to the pitch of the ball.

Even when you're leaving a ball, you should step across and guard your stumps and raise the bat to let the ball go through.

I'd just finished batting when the second disastrous thing happened, only it didn't seem that disastrous at the time. Henry Rossi turned up. Henry plays for Mudlarks. He's a good bat and he bowls medium-pace seamers. He came straight over to me as if he had something important to say.

"Are you looking for some new players, Hooker?"

"Why?"

Henry told me that there'd been problems at Mudlarks; the person in charge of the Under 13s had forgotten to register them for the League. I'd been wondering why Mudlarks weren't playing this year – they're one of the top teams.

"So some of us are trying to get games with other teams. Sam and I would like to play for Glory Gardens," said Henry.

Azzie and Clive are standing close to the wall in the slip-catching position and Cal and Erica throw tennis balls on to the wall from behind them. The catchers try to catch the rebounds and then flip the ball back over their shoulder to the catcher who throws again. You play in teams – a catcher and a thrower in each team – and the winner is the team to catch the most balls in five minutes. Then catchers and throwers change round and you start again.

"I don't know. We've got 12 or 13 players and you know Frankie's our keeper."

"Sam wouldn't mind not keeping wicket," said Henry. Sam Keeping's the best wicket-keeper I've ever seen. He even stands up to Bazza Woolf, Mudlarks' opening bowler who's nearly as quick as Marty.

"Well, maybe if we get some injuries or someone can't play," I began. Then I remembered that I wouldn't be playing next week.

"Let us know then," said Henry.

In the end he joined in our practice session and when he batted I couldn't help thinking what a difference he'd make to Glory Gardens. Just think, Henry opening the batting and Sam behind the stumps – with them we'd be favourites for the League, no question.

But we had a full side for next Saturday even with me out. So there was no point in thinking about it. And if Frankie hadn't hooked a ball into his face a few minutes later, that would have probably been the end of it.

Frankie was mucking about as usual telling Marty that he was bowling almost as slowly as Cal. Marty let fly at him with a really quick ball and it climbed on Frankie; it probably hit a bump because the grass nets are a bit rough in places. Frankie swung at it and got a top edge straight into his left eye. It started swelling up immediately and within minutes his eye was completely closed.

Kiddo took one look at it and decided to call Frankie's mum to take him to the hospital. "It's probably just bruised, but you can't be too careful with eyes," he said.

"Are you okay? Can you see anything, Frankie?" asked Jo, who was looking really worried.

"Don't tell me. I think I recognise that voice," said Frankie.

"Don't be stupid, Francis. Can you see out of your left eye?"

"No. But then it's shut, isn't it."

Their mum turned up and Jo went to the hospital with

Frankie. That meant that the selection committee after Nets was just Marty and me.

I told Marty about Henry Rossi and Sam Keeping.

"That's great," said Marty. "If Frankie can't play next week we can pick Sam as wicket-keeper."

"If we pick Sam we've probably got to consider Henry, too. And if we pick Henry we've got to drop someone."

"Well, it's obvious. We drop Ohbert," said Marty.

"Jo wouldn't like that," I said.

"She's not here."

"I'm not sure I like it, either."

"Look, if we want to win the League, we've got to pick the best team we can."

"But what if more of the Mudlarks want to play for us? When do we stop dropping Glory Gardens players?"

"We're not dropping a player, we're dropping Ohbert. We dropped him last week, didn't we?"

"But we sort of agreed that we'd pick him this week."

"You might have. I didn't and he played anyway."

I was getting a bit worried about the way things were going. But the problem was I wouldn't be playing; Marty was captain next Saturday and I didn't want to be too pushy about *his* team. So I let him have it his way. Anyway, it wasn't definite that Frankie was out.

So this was the team sheet that we pinned up on the notice board.

M Rose	F Allen
C Sebastien	T Vellacott
A Nazar	J Gunn
C da Costa	M Lear (capt)
E Davies	P Bennett – twelfth man
H Rossi	S Keeping – reserve if
T McCurdy	Frankie can't play

Ohbert had gone home but Henry Rossi was still there. "That's great," he said. "I can't wait to play. I won't let you down – promise."

Clive was dead pleased. "At last we're getting to be a real cricket team," he said. "But I can't understand why you don't pick Sam straight out as keeper. He's ten times better than Frankie."

But some weren't so happy – especially Tylan and Mack, too. I was surprised to hear Mack supporting Ohbert because he's so competitive and really likes to win. But he even offered to stand down and let Ohbert have a game. Mack's been playing for us for less than a year but it feels like he's been with us for ever. He's a great team player and everyone likes him. One of the good things about Mack is that he doesn't beat about the bush – he tells you exactly what he thinks. That's not to say he moans about things; he just comes out and says what's on his mind and that's it.

"The way I see it is that we've got a winning team and if it isn't broken you don't fix it," he said.

"But if Hooker can't play and Frankie's out what are we going to do?" asked Marty.

"All the more reason why Ohbert should play. He's stuck with us, so we should stick with him. He ought to play before me, by rights."

"But he's hopeless," insisted Marty. "And we want to win."

"It won't be like playing for Glory Gardens," said Tylan.

"Let's leave it there," said Mack. "I've had my say but in the end it's up to the selectors."

"Too right!" said Clive.

Cal hadn't said a word, so I asked him later what he thought.

"I'll tell you after Saturday's game," he said. And no matter how many times I asked him he wouldn't say any more.

Chapter Five

We got back from Uncle Pete's and Aunt Eileen's at 7 o'clock on Sunday evening and, almost before the car had stopped outside our house, I was ringing Cal's doorbell.

Cal opened the door.

"Did we win?" I asked.

"Yeah, easily."

"How many by? Who scored the runs? How many did we get?"

Cal laughed. "I knew you'd be like this, so I've brought the score-book home and the results of the other games and even a match report."

"What? You mean like in the newspapers?"

"Yeah. It was Jo's idea. She says she's going to write about all our games from now on and send the reports to the Gazette."

"They'll never put Under 13s games in the paper."

"You never know."

When we got to his room Cal showed me what Jo had written.

UNDER 13s LEAGUE
Waterville v Glory Gardens

Glory Gardens won the toss and batted first on a lively track. They lost early wickets to the bowling of Hanley and Calloway. Then Matthew Rose and Clive da Costa put on 36 quick runs for the third wicket before Rose was run out for 15. Da Costa went on to score a superb 46 before he was caught on the square-leg boundary going for his 50. Useful scores by Rossi (17 not out) and McCurdy (10) took the Glory Gardens total to 98 for six at the close of their 20 overs. The pick of the Waterville bowlers was Calloway with two for 14.

The Waterville innings got off to a disastrous start when Marty Lear and Jacky Gunn each took two wickets in their opening overs. Waterville recovered slightly from 3 for four to 14 for four but then another collapse put the game beyond doubt. Two wickets to Calvin Sebastien, including a brilliant caught and bowled, left the batting side struggling on 35 for seven. They were finally all out for 51 in the 17th over. In a fine display of wicket-keeping, Sam Keeping had four victims behind the stumps and gave away no byes.

GLORY GARDENS

M Rose	run out	15
C Sebastien	c Sleight b Calloway	2
A Nazar	lbw Hanley	0
C da Costa	c Blackett b Orde	46
E Davies	st Blizzard b Sleight	0
H Rossi	not out	17
T McCurdy	c Orde b Calloway	10
S Keeping	not out	0
Extras		8
		98 for six

WATERVILLE

B Hanley	b Lear	0
J Sleight	c Keeping b Gunn	0
J Blackett	lbw Lear	1
J Orde	st Keeping b Gunn	0
P Land	run out	14

M Calloway	c McCurdy b Sebastien	13
T Blizzard	c & b Sebastien	1
R Hellaby	c Keeping b Vellacott	7
P Neeves	b da Costa	4
D Ferreira	c Keeping b da Costa	5
B Love	not out	3
Extras		3
		51 all out

"Did you like that bit about a brilliant caught and bowled?" asked Cal. "It was going for four and I dived and caught it just with the ends of my fingers. Amazing."

"If you say so." I looked at the score-book again. "Frankie didn't play then?"

"No," said Cal. "Doctor's advice – the swelling hasn't quite gone down. He's okay though. He came along to watch and he made more noise than the 22 who were playing. It hasn't affected his voice."

I didn't say anything to Cal about Sam's wicket-keeping but I could tell what was on his mind. It was going to be hard to drop Sam after that performance.

"Clive was Player of the Match again, of course," said Cal.

"That's all right; he can wear Frankie's stupid cap for another week." I looked at the Glory Gardens bowling figures.

	OVERS	MDNS	RUNS	WICKETS
M Lear	4	0	9	2
J Gunn	4	1	11	2
C Sebastien	4	0	12	2
T Vellacott	2	0	10	1
H Rossi	2	0	6	0
C da Costa	0.5	0	2	2

"Erica didn't bowl?" I asked.

Cal wasn't giving anything away. He's a good friend of Marty's too and I knew that he wouldn't criticise the way he captained. "No, we didn't need her."

"Was she upset?"

"A bit quiet. But that may have been because she got a duck. Want to see how the other teams got on?" He gave me a sheet of paper with the results and League positions.

Arctics *lost to* Wyckham Wanderers by 2 runs
Waterville *lost to* Glory Gardens by 47 runs
Old Courtiers *beat* Croyland Crusaders by 4 wickets
Stoneyheath & Stockton *beat* Brass Castle by 20 runs.

	PLAYED	W	L	PTS
Glory Gardens	2	2	0	20
Wyckham	2	2	0	20
Arctics	2	1	1	10
Croyland	2	1	1	10
Old Courtiers	2	1	1	10
Stoneyheath	2	1	1	10
Brass Castle	2	0	2	0
Waterville	2	0	2	0

"All right," I said at last. "What are we going to do?"

"About?"

"About picking a team for Wednesday?"

"Oh, I forgot to tell you," said Cal with a grin. "Bazza Woolf wants to play for us. He came along to watch."

"It's not funny," I said.

"I know, I'm glad I'm not a selector."

"So tell me, who's available?"

"Everyone. Sam, Henry and Bazza from Mudlarks, all the regulars. Frankie's back . . . and Ohbert, of course. Oh, and I suppose *you* want a game this week?"

I counted them up. "That's fifteen players."

"Yeah, strength in depth! You'll either have to play fifteen a side or drop four. Perhaps you should ask for volunteers."

"And who would volunteer to drop out?"

"Clive perhaps?" said Cal with a wicked grin.

The next day at school, Jo, Marty and I got together after lunch to select the team.

Marty couldn't stop talking about the victory. "You should have seen Sam standing up to my bowling, Hooker. He was brilliant. And that stumping off Jacky. He took it down the leg side, didn't he, Jo?"

Jo nodded and frowned. It was as if Marty the Pessimist and Jo the Dynamo had swapped places.

"So who are we going to drop so that Hooker can play?" said Marty.

Jo looked at me but I didn't say anything.

"I reckon it'll have to be either Henry Rossi or Matthew – but they both scored runs and Erica didn't have a very good game."

"That's because you didn't give her a bowl," said Jo suddenly.

"Well I think Henry's a better bowler, don't you, Hooker?" said Marty.

"Since you ask, no." I said.

"Okay. Well what about dropping Matthew?" Marty suggested. "We've got enough batting without him grinding out the runs."

"Oh, I've had enough of this," said Jo. "How can you talk about dropping Matthew or Erica? And what about Francis and Ohbert?"

"I can understand you sticking up for Frankie," said Marty. "But face facts, Sam's a ten-times-better keeper. And we want to win the League, don't we? It'd be crazy to break up the team that's going to do it."

Jo turned to me. It was the moment I'd been dreading. "What do you say, Hooker? Do you want to win with a real Glory Gardens team or not?"

"This is my choice for Wednesday," I said, thrusting in front of them a sheet of paper on which I'd written the team

41

I'd been working on half of Sunday night.

Matthew Rose	Mack McCurdy
Cal Sebastien	Sam Keeping
Azzie Nazar	Tylan Vellacott
Clive da Costa	Jacky Gunn
Erica Davies	Marty Lear
Hooker Knight	

They both looked at it carefully. Marty spoke first.

"Okay, I still think Henry should play but I'll go along with that," he said.

"Well I won't," said Jo. "If you can't pick Frankie or Ohbert, you can do without me, too."

"Frankie'll be back," I said. "If he's fully fit at Nets on Saturday we'll pick him for the next game."

"I don't believe you, Hooker," said Jo coldly and she walked away.

I'd tried to come up with a team that both Jo and Marty would accept but it hadn't worked. And, to be honest, I hadn't really expected it to.

"Don't worry, Hooker. She'll come round," said Marty. Marty the Pessimist was hard to bear sometimes, but this new Marty was even worse.

Later that afternoon Frankie brought me a letter. "Beware, it's from the weird sister," he said.

To H. Knight, Captain of Glory Gardens.

Dear Hooker,
I am very sad to tell you that I am resigning as Secretary, Scorer and Selector of Glory Gardens C.C.

There's nothing personal about this but I think the Club is making some big mistakes. I can't do anything about it, so I'm resigning.

Yours sincerely
Jo Allen

"What's it say?" asked Frankie.

"She's resigned from Glory Gardens."

"Thought so. I've never seen her so miserable."

"Listen, I'm sorry you weren't picked for Wednesday," I said.

"Forget it," said Frankie. "I'll come along and score for you if you like. Don't suppose that'll please Jo – me messing up her beautiful score-book. I'd better do it in pencil."

I tried to explain to Frankie that this was only an experiment for one match but the more I said, the less convincing it sounded. And he kept saying "Don't worry, Hooker," which made it worse still because I knew he wanted to play.

"Mind you," he said finally. "After all this fuss, you'd better win."

Chapter Six

Arctics was an away game and out of town, so we went by car – or to be exact three cars: Kiddo's, Azzie's dad's and Dave Wing's. Wingy is the Priory Firsts' best fast bowler and he coaches us sometimes.

I hadn't had a chance to talk to Kiddo about the latest team selection but I thought he looked a bit surprised when he saw Sam Keeping waiting with us outside school.

We were late leaving because Tylan had gone missing.

"Maybe his dad's taking him," suggested Azzie.

"Funny thing," said Frankie. "He said to me, 'Have a good game' and then he went off and that was the last I saw of him."

"He'll be there," said Marty. "Tylan wouldn't miss a match without telling us."

In the end Kiddo said we couldn't wait any longer and we left without Tylan. On the way we picked up Matthew, Jacky, Mack and Clive who all go to schools on the other side of town. For once Clive was on time. He had his Player of the Match cap on and was trying not to look embarrassed wearing it in the street.

There was no sign of Tylan when we got to the ground, but Henry Rossi was there because no one had told him he wasn't playing. I'd forgotten. It's usually Jo who rings people up to remind them they're playing and Jo had been avoiding me since she handed in her resignation.

"Good thing you're here," said Marty to Henry. "It doesn't

look as if Ty's coming. You can play instead of him."

"Wait a minute," I said. "Frankie's twelfth man."

"But we don't want two wicket-keepers," said Clive.

"He's twelfth man, so he plays," I said. Clive didn't argue. I turned to Henry. "Sorry. But you know how it is." Henry's been captain of Mudlarks, so I thought he'd understand that mix-ups like this can happen in the best cricket teams. He didn't look pleased, though. Still, he stayed to watch the game and in the end he agreed to do the scoring for us. He sat next to Ohbert on a bench in front of Arctics' old, half-collapsed pavilion.

I don't know what Ohbert was saying to him but it was probably his usual gibberish. Each time I looked over towards them Henry seemed more and more puzzled, and he was combing his hair furiously.

Henry's tall and broad and he thinks he's good looking. He's got more clothes than the rest of Glory Gardens put together and his best friend is his comb; he probably combs his hair 3,000 times a day.

Ohbert, on the other hand, has never looked in a mirror in his life. He can't have because he couldn't look like he does if he used a mirror. I think he throws all his clothes up in the air in the morning and wears the first ones to land. Seeing Ohbert at school first thing is always a shock. Today he was in a mainly orange tee-shirt, which kept falling off his shoulders, and long pea-green shorts. Ohbert's so weedy that all his clothes look too big for him – except his old cricket kit which is three sizes too small. As usual he had his Walkman perched on top of his back-to-front baseball cap and he wasn't taking the slightest notice of the game.

They made a strange sight – Ohbert and Henry, sitting side by side on the bench by the boundary – and when Gatting waddled over and sat between them, they looked even odder. "Look, the Glory Gardens Supporters Club," said Cal. "Doesn't it make you proud."

I lost the toss and they batted. I told Sam to put on the

45

keeper's pads and put Frankie in the slips because Azzie, our usual slip specialist, is a lot quicker than Frankie in the field. Sam and Frankie immediately started talking and laughing like long lost friends.

It was a cold, windy evening and that was enough to get Frankie going. "This must be your sort of weather, mate," he said to the Arctics opening bat. "Suppose you've got your seal skins on underneath?"

Sam laughed loudly.

"Yeah, and I came here in my kayak and the polar bear's tied up behind the pavilion," said the Arctics opening bat who had heard a lot of 'Arctics' jokes. He didn't know that you shouldn't encourage Frankie.

"Which one can't you eat?" said Frankie. "An arctic roll, a penguin or a kayak?"

"A kayak?" said Sam.

"Right. Because you can't have your kayak and eat it. Get it?"

Sam fell about but the batsman pretended not to hear.

"Cool customers these Arctics," whispered Frankie to Sam and Sam laughed louder than ever.

I gave Mark the end with the wind behind him and he worked up a good pace. But it was Jacky, bowling into the wind, who caused the most trouble. He was swinging the ball away from the two right-handed openers and they couldn't lay a bat on him. I've never seen two batsmen play and miss so many times but neither of them got a single edge. We didn't take a wicket till the sixth over when one of the openers played over a straight one from Jacky.

Jacky got another one in his next over thanks to a lightning stumping by Sam backed up by the loudest appeal you've ever heard from Frankie.

"Sam Keeping, you're the best," said Frankie generously.

Jacky finished with amazing figures – four overs, two maidens, four runs, two wickets – and when he came off Arctics were 16 for two.

Although Marty bowled well he didn't take a wicket. He clean bowled one of the openers with a fast yorker but the umpire called a no ball. It was the only no ball of the innings so it was a bit of a shame.

Cal and Erica replaced Marty and Jacky and they didn't let Arctics off the hook. Cal had a hard, one-handed chance put down by Matthew at point and Erica, who was swinging the ball almost as much as Jacky, got an outside edge which flew to Frankie's left. He stuck out a hand and brought off a great reaction catch.

"Maybe it was a good thing you came along," he said to Sam, "or else Glory Gardens wouldn't have discovered the slip fielder of the century."

Sam laughed his head off.

In Erica's second over Marty made a horrible mess of a big towering catch at deep square-leg. The ball was in the air a long time and he got in position but then completely failed to get a hand on it as it came down. It was probably swirling about in the wind but he wasn't pleased with himself and nor was Erica.

"First you won't let me bowl, now you've cost me a wicket," she said to Marty who scowled and then looked away rather sheepishly.

Her next ball was driven hard along the ground to Mack's left at cover point. He swooped on it and it bounced forward out of his hand. The batsman called a sharp single. Mack's recovery was lightning. He gathered the ball and threw all in one movement. It crashed into the stumps – unbelievable, a direct hit with only one stump to aim at. The batsmen were left marooned in the middle of the pitch staring at the wrecked stumps and arguing which one of them was out. In the end the non-striker walked grumpily back to the pavilion.

The new batsman lashed his first ball straight at Mack and ran. "No!" the cry came from the other end, and he just had time to turn and watch the ball winging into Sam's gloves. Two run outs in two balls – and both to Mack.

47

Mack picks up and throws on the run. Look how he 'attacks' the ball. His hands are together with the fingers pointing down. From this position he can step forward and throw as his weight transfers from right to left foot.

At the half way stage Arctics were struggling on 25 for five.

Their skipper, Si McLachlan, who'd been the cause of both the run outs, hit a couple of solid blows off Cal. Then he skied one to mid-wicket where Mack made no mistake.

With four overs left they still had only 36 on the board. Time for the captain to have a bowl, I thought. I came on down wind and immediately got one to rear up and lob off the defending batsman's glove to Sam behind the stumps. It had probably hit a bump in the pitch – but who cared, it was another wicket.

Sensing that it was all or nothing the Arctics started to slog at everything. Two horrible swings to leg brought them four more runs but it couldn't last. You can't keep playing shots with your head in the air and get away with it. My next ball went past the bat and knocked out the middle stump.

I asked Mack to bowl at the other end, even though Clive was trying to catch my eye by wheeling his arm over and jumping up and down.

Marty got carted for the first four of the innings and then the tailender snicked one to Sam – it was well wide of his right hand and might have carried to Frankie at slip. Sam dived in front of Frankie. He got the ball in his outstretched glove but he couldn't hold on. Just as it was dropping to the ground he managed to knock it up again. And Frankie dived forward on his paunch and took the rebound.

"Put it there," said Sam.

"What a team! You know, I think I'm even more brilliant in the slips than behind the wicket," said Frankie, modest as ever.

Mack's next ball cannoned into the last batsman's pads as he stood plumb in front of his stumps and even Sid didn't hesitate giving lbw.

"Does that mean I'm on a hat trick with my first ball in the next match?" asked Mack.

"I suppose so," I said but I wasn't sure.

"Then you just wait. You'd better open the bowling with me."

"There's Ty," shouted Frankie suddenly. "Hey Ty, has your watch stopped?"

Tylan walked over and slapped Frankie on the back. "Well played," he said. "That was an outrageous catch."

"I got another one earlier," said Frankie. "But where have you been?"

"Oh, Dad got lost," said Tylan with a shrug.

"Tylan," said Frankie.

"Yeah?"

"What did you mean when you said to me have a good game? You knew I was only twelfth man."

"Well, I suppose I thought it was your turn to play," said Tylan.

"What you mean is you deliberately turned up late so that Frankie could play," said Jacky.

Tylan shrugged again.

"Is he crazy or what?" said Clive.

49

"Yeah, you wouldn't understand anyone doing something like that for a friend, would you," said Matthew suddenly. Everyone turned and looked at him because he's usually so quiet. He went bright red.

"Anyway, seems you managed okay without me," said Tylan. "Now let's make it three wins in a row."

HOME TEAM	ARCTICS	V	GLORY GARDENS	AWAY TEAM	AT	ARCTICS
					DATE	MAY 18th

INNINGS OF ..ARCTICS.. TOSS WON BY ARCTICS WEATHER WINDY

BATSMAN	RUNS SCORED	HOW OUT	BOWLER	SCORE
1 S. GOPOLAN	2.1.1.2.1	st KEEPING	GUNN	7
2 J. HODGE	1.1.1.1	bowled	GUNN	4
3 S. McLACHLAN	2.1.2.2.2	ct McCURDY	SEBASTIEN	9
4 T. PITMAN	1.1.2	ct ALLEN	DAVIES	4
5 T. PATTERSON	2	RUN	OUT	2
6 B. FANT		RUN	OUT	0
7 G. BOWSKY	1.2.1.4.1	NOT	OUT	9
8 P. MORGAN	1	ct KEEPING	KNIGHT	1
9 H. DUBON	2.2	bowled	KNIGHT	4
10 G. NOAKES		ct ALLEN	McCURDY	0
11 P. ST. HILL		lbw	McCURDY	0

FALL OF WICKETS

	1	2	3	4	5	6	7	8	9	10
SCORE	10	15	20	25	25	29	36	40	45	45
BAT NO	2	1	4	5	6	3	8	9	10	11

BYES		
LBYES	1.1.1.1	4
WIDES		
NO BALLS	1	1

TOTAL EXTRAS	5
TOTAL	45
FOR WKTS	10

SCORE AT A GLANCE

BOWLING ANALYSIS ⊙ NO BALL + WIDE

BOWLER	1	2	3	4	5	6	7	8	9	10	11	12	13	OVS	MDS	RUNS	WKT
1 M. LEAR	..2. / ..1.⊙	..1. / .1..	..2. / ..1	✕										4	0	11	0
2 J. GUNN	M M	M	.1W .2.	..W .1.	✕									4	2	4	2
3 C. SEBASTIEN	..1. / .1..	.2. / .1..	.22. / .W..	..2	✕									4	0	10	1
4 E. DAVIES	..2. / .W..	..1. / 2...	.... / .1..	..1 / 1...	✕									4	0	7	1
5 H. KNIGHT	W.. / 22W													1	0	4	2
6 T. McCURDY	.41 / WW													0.5	0	5	2
7																	
8																	
9																	

The scorecard of the Arctics innings, after Jo had rewritten it.

Chapter Seven

If we'd thought Arctics were going to be a walk-over, we soon got a different idea. They hadn't batted very well but their bowling quickly made up for it.

Their opening bowler was a real handful. He wasn't a typical fast bowler – in fact he was probably smaller than Jacky – and he wasn't particularly fast either, but he bowled a perfect length and he knew how to make full use of the uneven pitch. Like Jacky and Erica he bowled into the wind and he got the ball to swing.

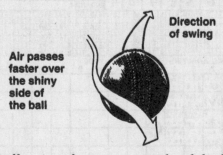

Direction of swing

Air passes faster over the shiny side of the ball

A cricket ball swings because one side of the ball is shiny and the other side rougher (that's why cricketers polish one side of the ball on their trousers). If the ball is released with the seam pointing down the leg side and the shiny side on the off-side, the ball will tend to swing into the right-handed batsman i.e. left to right. This is because the air passes more easily over the shiny side of the ball and is slowed down by the rough side; it creates a 'drag' on the ball as it moves in the air.

Matthew was the little opening bowler's first victim, a thin outside edge to the keeper. Then he got Azzie with a beauty which bounced and left him and flew to slip. That was two ducks in a row for Azzie. I knew his run of bad form wouldn't last – Azzie's a class player and he'll always score runs in the end – but he looked very depressed as he walked off.

Clive hit a beautiful off-drive for four and then he too got tied down by the bowling. Clive doesn't like bowlers to get on top and you could almost feel the pressure building up. Finally he went for a big swing at a full toss, missed and was clean bowled. I remembered Kiddo telling me that the ball he feared most was the loose one that came after you'd been tied down. You went for it greedily and ended up playing a stupid shot.

We were now 14 for three. And when Erica went cheaply, too – bowled off her pads, it was obvious we were going to struggle.

Cal hadn't been doing much more than keeping the ball out of his stumps and watching the wickets fall at the other end. But when I joined him at the wicket, he'd already decided that attack was the best form of defence.

"You get your eye in," he said, "and I'll see if I can push it along a bit. There are a few odd bounces at your end, so watch out."

I had three balls to face from Patterson, the little opening bowler, who was now in his last over. He'd already taken three of the four wickets. My plan was to see him off and then attack the new bowlers.

The first ball was well-pitched-up and I stretched as far forward as I could and missed it completely as it swung away from me. This wasn't going to be easy. The next was short. I got my bat on it and dropped it down at my feet. The last ball was just outside the off-stump and going away from me. I should have left it but it was a half-volley and I couldn't resist it. I launched into the drive. The ball took the edge and flew straight to their skipper, Si McLachlan, in the slips; he put down a sharp chance and we ran two.

53

Cal smirked and shook his head as if to say – call that getting your eye in? He then launched into the bowling with venom. Cal's very tall; he's got a long stride and he hits hard and straight. Two straight drives and an edge over slip brought us eight runs.

I went back to plan A and played the next over defensively. The new bowler was Si McLachlan himself. He was a bit slower than the opening bowler but every ball was on the stumps and all I could do was play them back defensively to the bowler.

Cal continued to attack the Arctics at the other end but then he drove over the top of a shooter and was bowled. He'd scored 14 out of our total of 30 for six. We still needed 16 runs to win the game, and apart from Mack there wasn't much batting to come.

Unfortunately, Mack tried to copy Cal before he'd settled in and he mis-hit the ball straight to mid-on. When Sam Keeping went next ball to another grubber, we were in really big trouble.

I always feel nervous when I see Frankie come to the wicket because you never know what he's going to do. Frankie's got a good eye but he can't resist having a slog. Sometimes it comes off – but it usually doesn't. It was the end of the over, so at least he didn't have to face the hat trick. I decided to try and keep as much of the strike as I could. There was still plenty of time and we needed only 13 runs but there was no point in saying that to Frankie. Frankie would play his own game whatever I said.

I got two from my favourite cut shot and a single down to third-man off the last ball of the over. Then I saw off Si's hat trick delivery and with the next ball I went for another cut but the ball was too far away from my body and I got it on the end of the bat. It lobbed in the air to point – and that was the end of my innings.

"Hard luck, Hooker," said Frankie. "Don't worry though. 10 to win. We'll knock those off in an over."

There was a full scale Glory Gardens row going on when I got back to the pavilion. It had all been started by Marty who was walking out to bat. It was no secret that Marty had never been keen on Ohbert playing for us, but now he'd told Jacky that he'd resign if Ohbert were ever picked again. "We've enough good players now with Henry and Sam – so why pick someone who's rubbish," he'd said.

Jacky and Matthew were on Ohbert's side and, of course, Clive supported Marty.

"Ohbert's a disgrace. He shouldn't be allowed on a cricket pitch," said Clive.

"You've got a short memory, Clive. There've been plenty of times when we've needed Ohbert. He's one of us – *and* he wants to play," said Jacky.

"Anyway, who says he's no good?" said Matthew.

"I do," said Clive. "And so does everyone who's got eyes."

"Well, yeah, I know he's not *very* good," said Matthew who was getting angry and doing a lot more talking than usual. "B . . . but I've seen him take one or two brilliant catches, and off your bowling, too."

"Pure fluke!" insisted Clive.

While everyone was talking about Ohbert, Ohbert just sat there, nodding his head from side to side to the incredibly loud buzzing sounds coming out of his Walkman. Why Ohbert wasn't completely deaf was one of life's great mysteries. He didn't, as usual, have a clue what was going on around him. Perhaps it was just as well.

"I think we should follow Ty's example and not turn up for the next game if Ohbert's not picked," said Jacky.

"That's crazy," said Azzie. "We want to win the League, don't we?"

"Oh no!" said Cal suddenly. Marty had gloved the ball to the keeper and was on his way back for a duck. We still needed 10 and Jacky joined Frankie at the wicket. This was our last chance – and a pretty slim one it was.

With Jacky out in the middle, the argument stopped apart

from the occasional moan from Tylan, "If we're so outrageously good without Ohbert, why are we on 36 for nine?"

It was the end of the over so Frankie faced the next ball. He took a wild swing and it missed his off-stump by a micro millimetre, but it beat the keeper, too, and went for two byes. Frankie was breathing hard after racing up and down the pitch but he laid into the next ball just the same. It squirted off a thick edge and just evaded short third-man's despairing dive. Two more runs.

"Come on, Frankie," shouted Tylan and Sam.

The fielders were becoming more and more excited and Si started moving them all about, which at least gave Frankie a chance to get his breath back. At last the bowler ran up. A full toss. Crack. The ball disappeared with two bounces over the square-leg boundary.

Now Glory Gardens were on their feet. Two to win. The argument forgotten, everyone was watching Frankie as he faced the fourth ball of the over. He went down the track to it and missed with his swing. The ball brushed off his thigh and the keeper stopped it as it went down the leg side. Frankie just had time to get back in his crease before the bails were whipped off.

A huge groan went up from Glory Gardens, then a sigh of relief as the umpire turned down the appeal.

Frankie missed the next ball, too, and it fizzed into the keeper's gloves. The bowler put his head in his hands. The final ball of the over was on middle stump and Frankie went for a reverse sweep! I couldn't believe it. I shut my eyes. And when I opened them the ball was racing along the ground fine of third-man to the boundary.

"Frankie, Frankie!" He was cheered all the way to the pavilion by the whole team. Si McLachlan looked shattered when he shook hands with me.

"He played his luck a bit," he said. "I thought we'd done enough."

"You never can tell with Frankie," I said.

We didn't bother to vote for the Player of the Match award. Tylan pulled the cap off Clive's head and crowned Frankie. Another great cheer went up for the hero of the hour. And to think, if it hadn't been for Tylan, he wouldn't have played at all.

The reverse sweep isn't in most coaching manuals. But if you practise it hard in the nets, it can be a useful surprise shot which will have slow bowlers pulling their hair out if you carry it off. But remember it's a dangerous shot because the ball can easily fly in the air off a top edge. Frankie lifts his bat over his left shoulder and plays the ball in front of his pad aiming in the direction of third slip. If you play this shot, it's better to choose a full length ball outside off-stump rather than play it off middle stump as Frankie does.

HOME TEAM ARCTICS	v	GLORY GARDENS	AWAY TEAM	AT ARCTICS DATE MAY 18th.		

INNINGS OF GLORY GARDENS	TOSS WON BY ARCTICS	WEATHER WINDY

BATSMAN	RUNS SCORED	HOW OUT	BOWLER	SCORE
1 M.ROSE	2 >>	ct Bowsky	PATTERSON	2
2 C.SEBASTIEN	1.1.1.4.2.2.1.2 >>	bowled	HODGE	14
3 A.NAZAR	>>	ct McLACHLAN	PATTERSON	0
4 C.DA COSTA	4 >>	bowled	DU BON	4
5 E.DAVIES	1	bowled	PATTERSON	1
6 H.KNIGHT	2.1.2.1.2.1 >>	ct ST. HILL	McLACHLAN	9
7 T.McCURDY	>>	ct FANT	McLACHLAN	0
8 S.KEEPING	>>	bowled	McLACHLAN	0
9 F.ALLEN	2.4.4	NOT	OUT	10
10 M.LEAR	>>	ct Bowsky	McLACHLAN	0
11 J.GUNN		NOT	OUT	0

FALL OF WICKETS

	1	2	3	4	5	6	7	8	9	10
SCORE	2	6	14	16	30	33	33	36	36	
BAT NO	1	3	4	5	2	7	8	6	10	

BYES	1.1.2		4	TOTAL EXTRAS	8
L BYES	1.1.1		3	TOTAL FOR	48
WIDES					
NO BALLS	l		l	WKTS	9

SCORE AT A GLANCE

BOWLER	BOWLING ANALYSIS ⊙ NO BALL + WIDE													OVS	MDS	RUNS	WKT
	1	2	3	4	5	6	7	8	9	10	11	12	13				
1 T.PATTERSON	..2 W..	..! W..	M	!!W ..2	X									4	1	7	3
2 H.DU BON	l..	..⊙..	V.	.4 .22	X									4	1	14	1
3 S.McLACHLAN	M	..2 !WW	.W											3	2	3	4
4 J.HODGE	!12 W..	..2 ..1	X											2	0	7	1
5 B.FANT	.24 ..4													1	0	10	0
6																	
7																	
8																	
9																	

The scorecard of the Glory Gardens innings, after Jo had re-written it.

Chapter Eight

Next day at school Kiddo told me that Azzie, Clive, Marty and I had been invited to play in the Under 13s Colts trials. There were two games; Clive and Marty were playing in the first one on Saturday afternoon and Azzie and I were in the second, a week later.

I didn't tell Cal immediately because I thought he might be disappointed that he hadn't been picked. But I needn't have worried. He found out from Marty and he immediately came looking for me.

"It's brilliant news, Hooker," he said. "Just make sure you get in the team. It'll be a disaster if Clive gets in and you don't."

"They should have picked you, too," I said.

"Oh, don't worry. They always pick fast bowlers and batsmen. We spinners never get a fair deal – even though we take most of the wickets."

"Oh yeah! Look at the averages then."

"I have. And I feel a bit sorry for Tylan and Erica – especially Erica. But I suppose it's too much to expect them to pick a girl for the Colts."

"She's better than most of the boys we play against."

"Yes, and any Glory Gardens player is good enough to play for the Colts."

"Except Ohbert."

"Except Ohbert," agreed Cal. "By the way, what side are you on in the civil war?"

"Civil war?"

"Where've you been? The Ohbertians versus the Martyites."

"The who versus the whats?"

"Marty and Clive want to drop Ohbert forever, and I think Henry and Sam are on their side – well they would be, wouldn't they? Jacky, Matthew, Tylan and Mack all say that if Ohbert's out they're out."

"You mean they won't play if Ohbert's not picked?"

"Precisely."

"That's blackmail! What about the others?"

"Erica's not a full Ohbertian but I think she's really on their side. Azzie's moving towards the Martyites – Marty's trying to brainwash him. Frankie doesn't seem to care one way or the other. And Ohbert doesn't even know what's going on."

"I can't believe he hasn't realised that everyone's talking about him," I said.

"Well if he has you can't tell," said Cal.

"That leaves you and me. What do you think?"

"It's difficult," said Cal. "I want Glory Gardens to stay like it is. But I want to win, too."

"That's the problem. But if we don't pick Ohbert half the team won't play."

"And if we do pick him we can't play Henry or Sam, and Marty and Clive will probably walk out. And that means our chances of winning the League go out of the window."

"So what do we do?"

"The problem is that without Jo on the Selection Committee, it's just you and Marty," said Cal.

"And if I agree with him I'm a . . . what d'you call it?"

"A Martyite."

"And if I don't we'll probably lose all our best players and just finish up with the Ohbertians. Oh, it's hopeless."

"Well, if you want to hear it, I've got a plan. But, I warn you, it's a bit way out. And if it goes wrong Glory Gardens will be right up the creek."

I listened to Cal's plan. At first I thought he'd gone off his rocker. But slowly I realised we hadn't got much choice. If we were going to stop the civil war, we had to do something fast. And Cal's plan was all we had.

We decided to put it into action at Nets on Saturday. But first we had to have Erica, Frankie and Ohbert on our side.

———————— • ————————

Clive didn't bother to turn up to Nets. He probably figured that, after Jo's resignation, we wouldn't be as strict on the rules as before, so he could just rest up for the Colts game in the afternoon. Tylan was on Knicker Rota and so that meant that one Ohbertian and one Martyite were missing. It couldn't have been better for The Plan.

"When shall I make my announcement?" I asked Cal.

"After Nets, I think," said Cal. "I've asked Jo to turn up and meet us in the pavilion."

"But she's an Ohbertian."

"Well sort of, but she's a Glory Gardener above all. And she's definitely on our side."

"I hope Ohbert remembers his lines," I said.

"So do I."

I couldn't concentrate properly on practice because I kept thinking about The Plan and everything that could go wrong with it. The civil war was showing no signs of coming to an end. Matthew and Jacky weren't even talking to Marty and Henry Rossi. And Marty was pushier than ever; I overheard him talking to Henry and Sam.

"You're both in the team for Wednesday," he said.

"But what about Hooker?" said Henry. "What does he think?"

"Oh, I shouldn't worry about Hooker," said Marty. "I'll talk him round."

That's what he thought! .

61

Kiddo split us into two groups. Azzie, Cal, Matthew, Henry and Ohbert practised how to play short-pitched bowling with Kiddo. He bounced a tennis ball in front of them and showed them how to decide whether to duck or sway out of the line of a bouncer.

Azzie shows how to sway out of the way of a bouncer. You only have a split second to deal with it and the most important thing is to watch the ball all the way and, if you're not playing it, to decide whether to duck or sway back. Notice Azzie's stance is side-on to the bowler, so he can easily sway forwards or back. Azzie is always very light on his feet – like a dancer – which helps him to adjust his position at the last minute.

Meanwhile both Sam and Frankie padded up as wicket-keepers and the quick bowlers bowled at them. Erica and Marty bowled in one net; Jacky and I in the other. Dave Wing watched us and he tried to get us bowling to an imaginary batsman's weaknesses.

"This batsman only plays half forward," he said. "What we call a shuffler. So you want to bowl well-pitched-up on middle stump – aiming to bowl him or get an lbw."

We bowled six balls pitched-up on the stumps and then Wingy introduced another sort of batsman, "This one's the batsman who gets on the front foot before the ball is bowled – you should bowl just short of a length to force him back and off balance."

We then had a new sort of fielding practice. Kiddo split us into two teams; one team with bats, the other without. At a signal, the fielding team takes turns to run, pick up a ball and run out the batsman. It works like this:

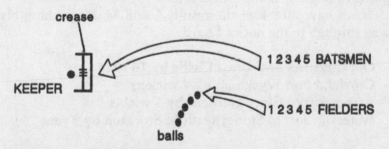

Fielder 1 runs, picks up a ball and throws at the stumps. At the same time, Batsman 1 runs to the popping crease. If he beats the throw he gets a point; if not, the fielders get a point.

Frankie was behind the stumps and he missed a throw from Marty. "Oh, send for the real keeper," said Marty. We all knew who he was talking about.

Ohbert was in Marty's team and when it was his turn to throw, he ran in, missed the ball completely and did a backward somersault as he tried to turn and pick it up.

"Zero. Null points," said Cal.

"But think of the degree of difficulty," said Frankie. "Must be 5 for technical merit."

"Hard luck, Ohbert," said Jacky who was in Marty's team, too.

"Hard luck?" sneered Marty turning away in despair. "He's an idiot."

And the civil war rumbled on till the end of Nets.

When we got back to the pavilion Jo was putting up the week's results on the notice board.

"I thought you'd resigned," said Azzie.

"I changed my mind after I saw the mess someone had made of my score-book," said Jo.

Henry Rossi blushed and started combing his hair nervously.

"His handwriting's so bad you can't even tell if he can spell," added Jo. "I had to redo it completely – and no one's going to touch it again. Understand?"

"Let's have a look at the results," said Marty pushing his way through to the notice board.

Old Courtiers *beat* **Brass Castle by 16 runs**
Croyland *beat* **Wyckham by 4 wickets**
Arctics *lost to* **Glory Gardens by 1 wicket**
Waterville *lost to* **Stoneyheath & Stockton by 9 runs**

	PLAYED	W	L	POINTS
Glory Gardens	3	3	0	30
Croyland Crusaders	3	2	1	20
Old Courtiers	3	2	1	20
Stoneyheath	3	2	1	20
Wyckham Wanderers	3	2	1	20
Arctics	3	1	2	10
Brass Castle	3	0	3	0
Waterville	3	0	3	0

"Jeez, we're top on our own!" said Mack.

"Wyckham got stitched!" cried Frankie. "What a blow for Katzy. Meeeiaow!"

Cal looked at me and nodded.

"Er, while we're all here – or nearly all," I said. "I've got something to say."

"Bit early for the victory speech!" said Mack.

"I've decided to stand down as captain," I said.

There was a silence. Then Marty spoke, "What do you mean, 'stand down'? You're giving up being captain?"

"Yes. I want to concentrate on my batting this season. And I think you should take over as captain – because you're vice captain already."

"Well, okay," said Marty a bit too keenly for my liking.

"He can't. It's not constitutional," said Jo.

"Not what?" asked Jacky.

"We've got to have an election," said Jo.

"Well, we'd better have it now," said Azzie. "We've got a team to pick for Wednesday and we need a captain."

"I propose Jacky," said Mack suddenly.

"Seconded," said Matthew.

"Well, I agree with Hooker, we should stick with the vice captain," said Azzie. "I propose Marty."

"I second Marty," said Henry, combing his hair.

"You can't second anyone," said Jacky. "You're not a full Glory Gardens player."

"Yes he is," stormed Marty.

Jo stepped in and put a stop to the row by saying it was all right for Henry to be a seconder. "Is that it?" she asked as she tore up pieces of paper for us to write our choices on. "Are there any more proposals?"

"I think Ohbert should be captain," said Frankie.

A couple of people giggled but Frankie didn't smile.

"You're joking aren't you," said Marty.

"Not a bit," said Frankie. "I propose Ohbert."

"And I'll second him," said Erica.

There was a gasp. "I think this club's going round the twist," said Marty. Even some of the Ohbertians looked shocked.

"I know Frankie can't help having a joke, but I'm surprised at you," said Azzie to Erica.

Erica shrugged and said nothing.

"Time to vote," said Jo.

We all wrote the name of our choice on the pieces of paper she gave us and put them in Frankie's Player of the Match cap.

Jo took the cap and went off to count the votes. She didn't take long.

"This is the result of the voting for captain of Glory Gardens Cricket Club," she said. "Jacky Gunn 3 votes; Marty Lear 4 votes; Paul Bennett 6 votes."

There was chaos.

"This can't be real," said Marty.

"I demand a recount," said Frankie.

"But you proposed Ohbert," said Azzie.

"Yeah, but I didn't think he'd get in," said Frankie with a grin.

"Do you want to be captain, Ohbert?" asked Erica.

Ohbert did a brilliant impersonation of someone emerging from a deep sleep, based on years of practice. "Me? Captain?" he said.

"Yes," said Jo.

"Does that mean I can play in the team?"

"'Fraid so," said Frankie.

"Oh but, all right then," said Ohbert and a silly smile spread over his face.

"And Marty's vice captain – because he got the second most votes," said Cal.

"I'm not going to be vice captain," said Marty. "And I'm not even going to play if he's captain."

"Oh but . . . M . . . M . . . Marty," began Ohbert.

"Then will you be vice captain, Jacky?" Jo asked.

66

"Er, I suppose so," said Jacky who looked completely amazed at everything that was going on.

"Well, I'm off to play a proper game of cricket," said Marty. "And if Ohbert's captain I'm not available on Wednesday." And he left.

"I want to know who voted for Ohbert," said Mack. "I certainly didn't."

"I did," said Ohbert.

"I thought you wanted him in the team, Mack," said Cal.

"Yeah, but there's a world of difference between having him playing and having him as captain."

Jo said it was time to pick the team for Wednesday, and off went the new selection committee: Jo, Jacky and Ohbert.

So far it all seemed to be working like a dream. Cal thought so anyway – when no one was looking he winked at me. But although The Plan was working, what was going to happen next? *We'd just made Ohbert captain of Glory Gardens!* But that was just the beginning of the story.

Chapter Nine

This was the team they picked:

P. Bennett (capt.)	A. Nazar
J. Gunn (v. capt.)	M. Rose
F. Allen	C. Sebastien
C. da Costa	T. Vellacott
E. Davies	Reserves:
H. Knight	H. Rossi
T. McCurdy	S. Keeping

Marty mostly kept out of our way for the next few days but he did speak to Jo. She told us he wouldn't change his mind. "He says he's never ever going to play for Glory Gardens again while Ohbert's captain – and that's definite."

He also told her that he'd taken three wickets in the Colts trial and Clive had scored 40 – as if we needed reminding how good they both were.

As I half expected, Clive pulled out of the team, too – I suppose he'd been brainwashed by Marty at the Colts game. Henry Rossi came in instead of him – the selection committee decided it was Henry's turn, because Sam had played in the last match.

"It would have been just as bad if we'd picked Ohbert and I'd carried on as captain," I said to Cal.

"Not quite," said Cal. "We've got Erica, Frankie and Jo on our side now – they all want the civil war to end. And if you'd picked Ohbert, we'd have lost Marty and Clive anyway and you'd have been blamed for it. This way you can still make a glorious comeback when Ohbert makes a mess of everything."

"But we don't want him to make a mess of it. We want to win."

"That's the hard bit. We've got to win but at the same time make sure everyone realises that we simply can't carry on with Ohbert as captain."

"How are we going to do that? Let's face it he doesn't know a single thing about cricket. So how can he be any good at captaining?"

"We'll have to teach him then," said Cal.

"You're joking?"

Cal grinned. "Look on the bright side. We haven't lost yet and we've still got eleven players . . . just."

We started 'coaching' Ohbert on Monday after school. It was hard to know where to begin. We started with the simplest things like tossing a coin but he wasn't even very good at that. Then we moved on to field placings and changing round bowlers and organising the batting order.

It was hopeless . . . as if we were talking in a foreign language. To make things worse Ohbert had a cold and he sniffed non-stop while we were talking to him. He showed a brief interest in the fielding positions which made him laugh like silly mid-off and long-leg and then his eyes clouded over and we knew his brain had drifted away again. He couldn't even seem to understand simple rules like changing the bowlers after four overs. When he said, "How many balls are there in an over, Hooker?" I realised that we were just wasting our time. We'd never educate Ohbert in a million years.

"He's got the concentration of a gnat," said Cal despairingly as Ohbert wandered off to look for his Walkman.

"I can't imagine how you ever thought we could win a single game with him in charge," I said.

Cal shrugged. For once even he looked beaten.

"We'll just have to stick to the most important things," I said. "Perhaps we could write down some lists for him to use. At least he can read."

"I suppose it's worth a try," said Cal.

We helped Ohbert write down the batting order on a piece of paper and told him to give it to Jo before the game. Then we told him to call heads and bat if he won the toss. But the biggest problem was what to do about field placing and bowling changes. We couldn't talk to him on the field because then the Martyites and Ohbertians would guess that something fishy was going on. So we drew four lots of field placings for him and we numbered them with a big 1, 2, 3 and 4 in the corner, like this.

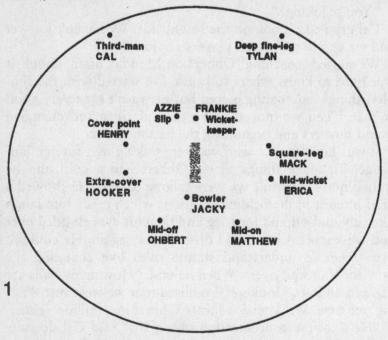

Woodcock Lane end

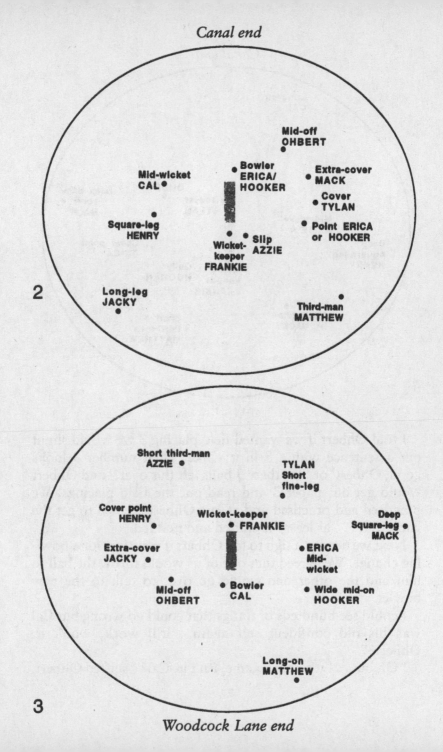

Canal end

2

Mid-off
OHBERT

Mid-wicket
CAL

Bowler
ERICA/
HOOKER

Extra-cover
MACK

Cover
TYLAN

Square-leg
HENRY

Point ERICA
or HOOKER

Wicket-
keeper
FRANKIE

Slip
AZZIE

Long-leg
JACKY

Third-man
MATTHEW

3

Short third-man
AZZIE

TYLAN
Short
fine-leg

Cover point
HENRY

Wicket-keeper
FRANKIE

Deep
Square-leg
MACK

Extra-cover
JACKY

ERICA
Mid-
wicket

Mid-off
OHBERT

Bowler
CAL

Wide mid-on
HOOKER

Long-on
MATTHEW

Woodcock Lane end

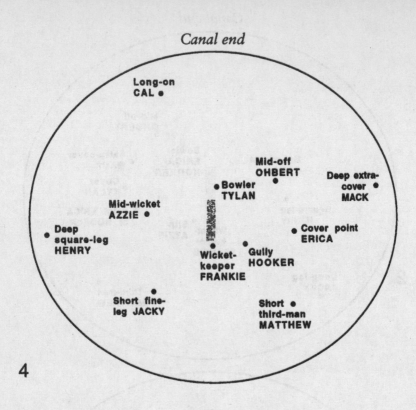

Canal end

Long-on
CAL

Mid-off
OHBERT

Bowler
TYLAN

Deep extra-
cover
MACK

Mid-wicket
AZZIE

Deep
square-leg
HENRY

Cover point
ERICA

Wicket-
keeper
FRANKIE

Gully
HOOKER

Short fine-
leg JACKY

Short
third-man
MATTHEW

4

I told Ohbert if we wanted field placing 3 we would shout out a sentence with a 3 in it – like 'Their number 3 looks good, Ohbert' or 'Are there 3 balls left this over?' and Ohbert would get out paper 3 and read out the field placings. We practised and practised and at last Ohbert seemed to get the hang of it . . . at least, he sniffed and nodded.

Next we needed a sign to tell Ohbert it was time for a bowling change. We agreed that one of us would throw the ball to him and the other one would go over to talk to the new bowler.

I could see hundreds of things that could go wrong but Cal was his old confident self again. "It'll work, won't it, Ohbert?"

"Oh but . . . it's only a game, isn't it, Cal?" sniffed Ohbert.

72

At last, Wednesday evening arrived. Most of us went straight to the Priory Ground after school and spent half an hour in the nets before Old Courtiers arrived. We'd played them and beaten them at the end of last season when they were League champions. But this was a completely new team to us. All the sides we played last year were a year older than us but now we were playing against teams of our own age.

Their captain came over and introduced himself. "I'm Rick Mattis. Who's your captain?"

"This is Ohbert," said Frankie.

"Oh really," said Rick, looking Ohbert up and down. Ohbert was listening to his Walkman and he grinned back vacantly.

"Shall we go and toss, then . . . er, Ohbert," shouted Rick.

"Oh but, what?" said Ohbert.

Eventually they set off for the middle; the tall figure of Rick Mattis striding out ahead and Ohbert bobbing up and down behind him like a badly trained puppy. Every now and again Ohbert would break into a trot to catch up. When they got to the middle, Rick Mattis had a close look at the pitch and then threw a blade of grass up in the air to check the wind direction. Ohbert did the same. Then Ohbert fumbled in his pockets for the 50p coin Cal had lent him. He struggled and struggled to get it out of his trousers and then it took him three goes to toss it properly. In the end he lost the toss and Rick Mattis put us in. That was probably a good thing; our best chance was to make a big score and hope that we could still hold them, whatever mess Ohbert made of captaining us in the field.

The first crisis came when Ohbert discovered he'd left all his lists at school. That meant he had to make up the batting order from memory. The list he gave Jo was just a jumble of names as they came into his head.

M Rose	P Bennett
E Davies	T McCurdy
H Knight	H Rossi
C Sebastien	J Gunn
F Allen	T Vellacott
A Nazar	

Tylan and Henry weren't very pleased about being right down the order but my biggest worries were Azzie at six, below Frankie, and Ohbert at seven. How could the idiot even think of playing himself any higher than eleven?

Erica and Matthew put on 16 for the first wicket against some accurate but not very penetrating bowling. I didn't see much of their batting because I was helping Ohbert to write out the field placings again. I saw Erica get out, though. She was caught by the keeper playing a fine glance down the leg side – it was a bit unlucky getting a touch but it was a great catch.

I was next in. I got off the mark with my first ball – a nicely timed push on the leg side.

Matthew and I agreed that I would try and push the scoring along and he'd take every single he could. I felt we should aim for a hundred to overcome the 'Ohbert effect' in the field – so we now needed to score between five and six an over.

Matthew tried a short single too many and ran himself out and in came Cal. He immediately played outside a good off-break and was bowled first ball. Frankie had three heaves: missed the first; squirted the second over slip for two and was caught at point off the third. That brought Azzie to the wicket.

"I can't get used to coming in at 29 for four," he said. I could see he was quite nervous which was unusual for Azzie but a run of bad scores can easily knock your confidence. He pushed half forward and missed his first delivery completely.

A wild swing at the second gave him a single off an inside edge that must have grazed his leg stump.

At the end of the over I met him in the middle.

"I'm going to attack these two," I said. "The medium-pacer's quite accurate and the spinner's turning it a bit. But if I get out, make sure you're still there at the end. We haven't got a lot of batting to come."

Azzie calmed down a bit. He watched the bowling carefully and when I got the strike I managed to keep the score moving, but at the half way stage we only had 35 on the board.

Azzie pushed a single off the first ball of the spinner's next over. Then I got a full toss which I pulled to leg for four. Two twos through the covers both nicely timed and I was beginning really to enjoy myself. I was seeing the ball very well by now. I even spotted that the fifth ball was a slower delivery, but I couldn't resist it. I swung it to leg and got a top edge. The ball went straight up in the air and the keeper ran round in front of me and took an easy catch. I'd scored 20.

As I walked off I met Ohbert coming the other way. It was hard to take the game seriously when Ohbert came in fifth wicket down.

"Well batted, Hooker," he said as we passed. Just for a moment I had the nasty feeling that Ohbert was beginning to believe in himself as captain of Glory Gardens.

He forgot to take guard; stood about a foot outside leg stump and looked at the spinner who ran in. Before the ball had left the bowler's hand Ohbert lunged forward to play his favourite forward defensive shot. It was a slow, short delivery and it bounced up and hit him on the nose. Play stopped for a few minutes while Ohbert rubbed and sniffed then he walked out to the middle of the wicket and tapped the pitch down with his bat.

"Outrageous!" said Tylan. "I think Ohbert's found a mole."

"I wish he'd fall down a mole hole," said Jacky.

Ohbert strutted back to his crease and stood waiting for the next ball to be bowled. But he hadn't noticed that it was the end of the over and the wicket-keeper grinned back at him from the other end.

The next two overs were amazing. First of all Azzie played the best timed cover drive I'd ever seen, all along the ground for four. A delicate late cut should have brought him three runs but Ohbert fell over in the middle of the second and only just got up in time to avoid being run out. At least it meant that Azzie kept the strike and he drove the fifth ball of the over hard back at the bowler who stuck out a boot and deflected it. It ran on, hit Ohbert's bat, bounced off his head and over the stumps. Ohbert watched it as Azzie called desperately for a single. Just in time he turned and ran to the other end nearly bumping into Azzie on the way. That left him with one ball of the over to face.

He played another slow, stylish forward defensive and the ball bounced off the handle of the bat and lobbed over the keeper's head for a single.

Old Courtiers were beginning to tear their hair out. They had Azzie at his most brilliant at one end and Ohbert at his worst at the other – but they couldn't get him out.

The spinner bowled to Ohbert. Ohbert played his other shot – the Ohfensive, we call it – a sort of short arm, cross-bat jab. The ball missed the bat, missed Ohbert, missed the stumps by a whisker, missed the keeper and went through for a bye.

Azzie cracked two fours in succession off the spinner – a straight drive back over the bowler's head and then, when he dropped short, a pull for four past square-leg. Next ball he was dropped at deep mid-wicket going for another big hit – he skied it and it wasn't an easy catch but the fielder made a real mess of it. They should have run two but Ohbert stopped to watch the catch.

Ohbert took guard again. 2 was already his third highest score ever for Glory Gardens. Now he tried a new shot in the Ohbert repertoire. I think it was supposed to be a copy of

Frankie's reverse sweep but it looked more like someone trying to toss a pancake with a cricket bat. Somehow he managed to make contact with the ball and it spooned up in the air exactly between silly mid-off and the bowler. They both dived for it, collided and the ball rolled away for a single.

Frankie was now on his feet cheering every ball. "Come on, Ohbert. Ohbert for England." He didn't seem at all embarrassed that Ohbert had now scored more than him.

Sadly though, it was Frankie's cheers which brought about the end of Ohbert's great innings. Ohbert was so busy listening and waving to Frankie that he took no notice of Azzie calling for a single off the next ball and they both found themselves at the bowler's end looking at each other. The keeper took off the bails and that was the end of a fine stand of 19. Ohbert had scored 3 – but he walked off to loud applause and whistles from Glory Gardens and a lot of grumbles from Old Courtiers.

"Some people don't get that much luck in a lifetime," said the fielder on the boundary in front of us.

We were 63 for six. Mack lost his leg stump going for a big off-drive and Henry Rossi went out to bat. I don't think he was very pleased to be batting at nine and to make things more difficult for him, he lost Azzie almost immediately – bowled by the spinner off an inside edge as he stepped back for a big cut.

At 68 for eight we needed to make sure we lasted out the remaining five overs. Henry got the message and he and Jacky just pushed the singles for a time without taking too many risks.

With two overs to go we had 77 on the board. Jacky went for a huge leg side swing in the next over and was caught at square-leg. But Henry and Tylan saw out the overs. We finished on 83 for nine.

Kiddo was quite pleased. "They bowled pretty well, kiddo," he said to me. "83 is not a bad total."

"Remember we haven't got Marty and Clive," I said.

"No," said Kiddo. "I've been meaning to ask you about that. And something else . . . er, why on earth is Paul Bennett captain today?"

There was no real answer to that, so I just said, "Everyone voted for him."

Kiddo scratched his head, sighed and walked off to look for Gatting who was busy digging up something under the pavilion steps.

HOME TEAM	GLORY GARDENS. V OLD COURTIERS .TEAM	AWAY	AT EASTGATE PRIORY DATE MAY 25TH

INNINGS OF .GLORY GARDENS..... TOSS WON BY O.C... WEATHER Cloudy

BATSMAN	RUNS SCORED	HOW OUT	BOWLER	SCORE
1 M. ROSE	1·2·1·2·1·1·1	RUN	OUT	9
2 E. DAVIES	1·1·1·1·1·2	ct WHITE	JOURDAIN	8
3 H. KNIGHT	2·2·1·3·2·2·4·2·2	ct WHITE	BENNETTO	20
4 C. SEBASTIEN		bowled	BENNETTO	0
5 F. ALLEN	2	ct MATTIS	BENNETTO	2
6 A. NAZAR	1·4·2·1·4·4·1·2·1	bowled	BENNETTO	20
7 P. BENNETT	1·1·1	RUN	OUT	3
8 T. McCURDY	2	bowled	AGNEW	2
9 H. ROSSI	1·1·1·1·2·1	NOT	OUT	8
10 J. GUNN	1·1	ct SINGH	MATTIS	2
11 T. VELLACOTT	1·1·1	NOT	OUT	3

FALL OF WICKETS										BYES	1·1·1			4	TOTAL EXTRAS	6
SCORE	16	27	27	29	44	63	68	68	77	10	LBYES	1·1			2	TOTAL FOR	83
BAT NO	2	1	4	5	3	7	8	6	10		WIDES / NO BALLS					WKTS	9

SCORE AT A GLANCE

BOWLER	BOWLING ANALYSIS ⊙ NO BALL + WIDE													OVS	MDS	RUNS	WKT
	1	2	3	4	5	6	7	8	9	10	11	12	13				
1 R. MATTIS	·:1 ·1·	1·1 ·2	X	1·· 1··	··1 ·2· W									4	0	10	1
2 M. JOURDAIN	1··	1·1	2·· 2·	··1 13·	X									4	0	13	1
3 B. COOKSON	1·2 ··1	··1 ·2·	··1 ·22	4·2 11	X									4	0	18	0
4 J. BENNETTO	W·2 W·1	142 2W·	·44 11·	W·1	X									4	0	24	4
5 D. AGNEW	·21 2W·	··1 ··1	1·1 1··	1·1 11·										4	0	12	1
6																	
7																	
8																	
9																	

Chapter Ten

I was now getting increasingly worried about Ohbert. Something about the way he led us out into the field made me feel very uneasy. He kept smiling – but it wasn't his usual stupid smile; he looked sort of pleased with himself. It was bad enough that Ohbert was hopeless but if he ever started to believe he could really be captain it would be a disaster. Cal noticed it, too.

"I think Ohbert's gone power crazy," he said.

To begin with things went quite well. Ohbert read out Fielding Plan 1 which Cal had redrawn for him and he opened the bowling with Jacky who got a wicket in his first over – the thinnest of snicks through to Frankie behind the stumps.

Then Ohbert brought Tylan on to bowl at the canal end. We had told him to open with Erica or me but Tylan wasn't such a bad choice. I think Tylan had probably been talking to Ohbert and had persuaded him to give him an early bowl.

"Is that *four*, they've scored, Ohbert?" asked Cal in a loud voice.

"No two," said Tylan.

"I think it's three," said Frankie.

Cal looked determinedly at Ohbert. "I'm sure it's *four*." But Ohbert was already reading out Plan 2 and so Tylan found himself bowling to a medium-pace bowler's field with no mid-on and six on the off-side.

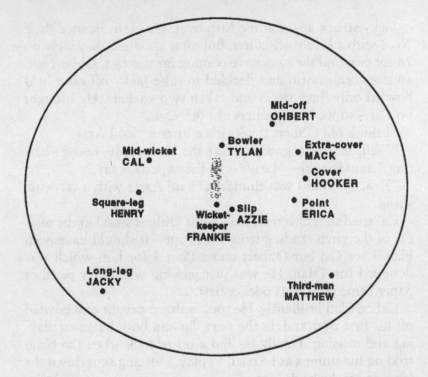

Ohbert even tried to send Tylan into the covers until he reminded him that he was bowling. The worst thing about the field placing was the wasted fielders in the deep behind the stumps and, with Tylan pitching his leg-breaks on or just outside leg stump, there were hundreds of gaps. Rick Mattis, their captain, soon spotted them and started running the ball down to fine leg or pushing it to mid-on and taking a quick single.

The score-board was rattling along and Cal and I began to realise that Ohbert really wasn't taking any notice of us whatsoever.

"I can't think of any more sentences with four in them," said Cal despairingly.

"Don't waste your breath," I said. "The stupid idiot's forgotten everything we told him."

Jacky struck again in the fifth over. He clean bowled their No.3 with a lovely off-cutter. But after six overs they were on 28 for two and the runs were coming far too fast. Ohbert had another brainstorm and decided to take Jacky off after he'd bowled only three overs and taken two wickets. He brought on Cal – so we had spinners at both ends.

"I think old Ohbert thinks it's a turner," said Azzie.

"Well, he had a good look at the pitch while he was batting," said Frankie. "Leave it to the experts, I say."

"Exactly what I was thinking," said Azzie with a sarcastic shrug.

Cal tried to set his own field – but Ohbert stood in the middle of the pitch reading from his script – it should have been Plan 3 for Cal but Ohbert chose Plan 4 for him which was designed for Tylan. He was just picking whichever piece of paper came out of his pocket first.

Cal bowled brilliantly. He took a sharp caught and bowled off his first over and, in the next, he had both batsmen playing and missing. Finally he had a bit of luck when the No.6 trod on his stumps as he tried to play a forcing shot down the leg side off the back foot.

Ohbert tried to give Tylan a fifth over and old Sid had to tell him that he was only allowed four. So Ohbert turned to Henry Rossi who just happened to be walking by at the time.

"Oh but, Henry," he said, "do you want to bowl?"

Henry's not a bad bowler but I was now seriously worried that Ohbert had gone into orbit and completely forgotten about Erica and me. I kept throwing the ball to Ohbert as we'd planned and Erica must have been wondering why Cal was spending so much time talking to her.

Henry's first over was directed too far down the leg side and Rick Mattis took full advantage of it with a four over square-leg and a sweep for two.

Frankie had a word with Cal at the beginning of the next over and I watched carefully to see what they'd planned.

The first two balls were pitched-up to the batsman,

drawing him forward on his front foot. Then a slow, slightly shorter one brought him down the wicket, driving over Cal's head for two. Another well-pitched-up ball drew the batsman forward. Then Cal bowled the quicker one outside the off-stump. The batsman came out for it, missed and Frankie whisked off the bails – he was stumped by a yard.

Cal's quicker ball is what he calls his 'undercutter'. He bowls it by keeping the arms and wrist a bit lower and his hand cuts underneath the ball. The ball pushed through like this often lands on the polished part rather than the seam and it skids off the pitch and surprises the batsman. Notice he's also bowling wide of the crease to change the angle and line of the delivery.

"Brilliant," yelled Frankie. "Worked like a dream!"

"I was surprised you managed to catch it," said Cal. "You've dropped most of the others."

"Well stumped, Frankie," said Ohbert.

"Thank you, Ohbert," said Frankie. "It's all going to plan, isn't it?"

"Oh but, I think so, Frankie."

"God help us," said Cal.

The 50 came up in Henry's next over but we got a wicket, too. Rick Mattis ran the ball out to Mack who by now was fielding in the unusual position for him of third man. Rick set off for a run, then he saw Mack coming in fast and shouted, "No." The non-striker turned, slipped and Mack sent in a low return to the bowler's end. Henry just managed to get back behind the stumps in time to catch it and knock off the bails. Up went Sid's finger.

They had 53 on the board after twelve overs. So they needed less than four an over. It was true they only had four wickets left but unfortunately one of them was Rick Mattis who was batting brilliantly on 31.

The new batsman came out and I could see from the way he was carrying his bat that he was a left-hander. Cal noticed, too. "Left-hander, Ohbert," he said.

"Is that good, Cal?"

"I mean, shouldn't the field change round?"

"Oh but, they'll be all right," said Ohbert, pretending to understand. So Cal bowled with a short square-leg and a leg slip as he turned the ball away from the left-hander. Unbelievably he managed to bowl a maiden. His final figures were amazing – three wickets for 5.

Henry's third over cost another six runs. Matthew dropped a low chance in the covers but it wasn't easy and Matthew only fields there when Ohbert's captain so he probably wasn't used to the angle or the speed of the ball. At the end of Henry's over we all looked at Ohbert to see who he would bring on at the Woodcock Lane end. He had a worried look on his face and he was swinging his arm around – for one terrible moment it looked as though he himself was going to bowl. Then suddenly his face brightened as he saw Cal jumping up and down next to Erica and he lobbed the ball in her direction. Erica ran about ten yards to her left and picked it up.

"Want me to bowl, Ohbert?" she said.

"Oh but, yes please, Erica," said our captain.

"Can I have a long-off and a deep square-leg," said Erica.

"Is it on here?" asked Ohbert, showing Erica one of his plans. By now he was completely confused.

"Yes," said Erica.

"That's all right then," said Ohbert. "Try and get a wicket."

"That's what I call leadership," said Frankie to Azzie. "I think he's really got the hang of the job now."

Erica was bowling at Rick Mattis. She kept the ball up to Rick – in the block hole on middle and leg stumps – and she bowled four dot balls in a row before he squeezed one down to long-leg. Only three runs came off the over. Henry's last over was as expensive as all his others but he nearly took Rick's wicket. Mack made an amazing attempt to take a catch off a skied top edge. The ball flew over his head and he ran towards the boundary. It was falling beyond him but he dived forward as the ball came over his shoulder and grabbed it in one hand, inches from the ground – but as he hit the deck it rolled out.

I glanced up at the score-board at the end of Henry's spell. 68 for six. They needed 16 off four overs. It was going to be close.

Rick Mattis crashed Erica through the covers for four in the next over but she hit back getting the other batsman lbw playing a sort of swish across the line.

At the end of her over Ohbert walked up to me. "Oh but, Hooker. I'm really sorry."

"What for?"

"I forgot you could bowl."

"Oh really?"

"Do you want a go now?"

"Yes, please."

"Oh that's good."

I had two overs and I had to make them both count.

My first ball was short and Rick Mattis pulled it hard but Cal, running flat out round the mid-wicket boundary, managed to cut it off and save two runs.

The next was well-pitched-up to Rick and he drove it hard back at me. The ball never got more than a foot off the ground. I threw myself to my right and – smack – it hit the palm of my right hand and stuck. I jumped up and threw the ball high in the air.

"Amazing! He can catch after all," said Frankie, rubbing his eyes in disbelief.

"Good catch," said Rick grudgingly as he walked off. I watched his score go up on the score-board. 48. My catch had cost him his 50.

Two more runs came off the over. That took them to 78. Six to win and two overs left. Frankie dropped a fairly easy one off the first ball of Erica's next over. Then he let through two byes. But otherwise Erica kept it very tight and there was only one run off the bat. They needed three from my last over.

I bowled a yorker which was dug out for a single. The next was edged just past Frankie's diving hand for another run. The scores were level. I had to take a wicket to save the match. I went round the wicket and decided to risk a disguised slower delivery from wide of the crease. The batsman swung at it and missed completely. It bounced over the stumps and Frankie stopped it with his pads and there was no run.

"Oh well done, fat man, you stopped one," said Cal to Frankie sarcastically. "Now try catching it for a change."

Three balls to go. My next one was quick. Pitched on a good length, it nipped in between bat and pad and over went the middle stump. 83 for nine and two balls to go.

By now I'd forgotten Ohbert was captain. I brought all the fielders in to save the single and went back to bowling over the wicket. The No. 11 batsman played his first delivery straight to Azzie at silly mid-on. No run.

I decided to bowl the last ball of the innings short of a length on the off-stump. If the batsman missed it we tied. If he hit it I had to have fielders in the right place to stop the single. I moved Cal down to fly slip and Erica to backward point. I looked at the empty leg-side boundary – no good worrying about that, if he hit it high on the leg side they'd won.

I bowled, a bit wider than I intended, and the batsman got an edge and ran. The ball went all along the ground, fast to Cal's left. He dived, rolled over and threw to Frankie. The throw was wide of the stumps but Frankie gathered it and flung himself at the wickets. He beat the diving batsman by a couple of feet.

We'd tied the match.

Everyone, the batsmen included, looked exhausted. Frankie rushed over to Cal and tried to lift him in the air but couldn't get him off the ground.

"What a throw, big man," he said.

"And what a take," said Cal. "Maybe you'll make a wicket-keeper after all."

We voted Cal Player of the Match. Without Ohbert we'd have won but a tie was a fair result. Rick Mattis came out of the pavilion to shake Ohbert's hand.

"Is that the finish, then?" said Ohbert.

"Outrageous," sighed Tylan.

HOME TEAM: GLORY GARDENS V OLD COURTIERS — AWAY TEAM

AT EASTGATE PRIORY **DATE** MAY 25TH

INNINGS OF OLD COURTIERS   **TOSS WON BY** O.C.   **WEATHER** CLOUDY

BATSMAN	RUNS SCORED	HOW OUT	BOWLER	SCORE
1 D.CHOWDHURY	2	ct ALLEN	GUNN	2
2 R.MATTIS	1·2·1·2·1·2·1·1·1·1·2·1·3·1·4 2·(26)·1·2·2·1·2·2·2·1·1·1·4·1·2	c & b	KNIGHT	48
3 D.AGNEW	1·1	bowled	GUNN	2
4 N.PETTIT		c & b	SEBASTIEN	0
5 A.WHITE	1·1	hit wkt.	SEBASTIEN	2
6 A.MELLON	1·1·2	st ALLEN	SEBASTIEN	4
7 B.COOKSON	1	RUN	OUT	1
8 C.LYNCH	1·2·1·1	lbw	DAVIES	5
9 P.SINGH	1·1·1	bowled	KNIGHT	3
10 M.JOURDAIN	1·1	RUN	OUT	2
11 J.BENNETTO		NOT	OUT	0

FALL OF WICKETS

	BYES	2·1·1·2			6	TOTAL EXTRAS	14

SCORE	1	2	3	4	5	6	7	8	9	10	LBYES	1	TOTAL	83
	2	21	29	36	47	51	74	76	83	83	WIDES	1·1·1·1 4	FOR	10
BAT NO	1	3	4	5	6	7	8	2	9	10	NO BALLS 1·1·1	3	WKTS	

SCORE AT A GLANCE

BOWLER	SOWLING ANALYSIS ⊙ NO BALL + WIDE													OVS	MDS	RUNS	WKT
	1	2	3	4	5	6	7	8	9	10	11	12	13				
1 J.GUNN	··2·2· ·W·⊙1·⊙·	1·W· ·1	✕											3	0	9	2
2 T.VELLACOTT	1·1 +1·	2·1 +1·	2·1 +·	+· 3·	✕									4	0	21	0
3 C.SEBASTIEN	··W·· ·1·	··1 ·N6	··2 ·1	M	✕									4	1	5	3
4 H.ROSSI	10·· ·2·	1·1 2·2·	1·1· 122·	121 1·1										4	0	26	0
5 E.DAVIES	··· ·21	··4 ···	··· ··1											3	0	9	1
6 H.KNIGHT	2W1·· ··1W·	1·1 W··												2	0	6	2
7																	
8																	
9																	

Chapter Eleven

Wyckham Wanderers *beat* Waterville by seven wickets
Brass Castle *beat* Arctics by 14 runs
Stoneyheath & Stockton *lost to* Croyland by 8 runs
Glory Gardens *tied with* Old Courtiers

	PLAYED	WON	LOST	TIED	POINTS
Glory Gardens	4	3	0	1	35
Croyland	4	3	1		30
Wyckham	4	3	1		30
Old Courtiers	4	2	1	1	25
Stoneyheath	4	2	2		20
Arctics	4	1	3		10
Brass Castle	4	1	3		10
Waterville	4	0	4		0

The tie had cost us 5 points but we still stayed top of the League and we were the only team who hadn't lost a game. How long would that last though, with Ohbert in charge?

Azzie and I didn't go to Nets on Saturday morning because the Colts trial was switched from the afternoon to the morning. Azzie's dad took us along to the county ground for the game.

Our side batted first. Azzie was No.3 and I was 4. The county ground was enormous and the changing rooms were the poshest I'd ever seen. I'd never felt so nervous in my life.

We were sitting waiting to bat when Azzie said, "You know

what, Hooker? We'll never win the League. Not with Ohbert as captain."

"Well, we voted for him."

"That's what I can't understand. I didn't vote for him – and I don't suppose you did. So how come he got elected?"

"Who knows?" I lied.

"But what I really can't work out is why you resigned."

"Because of the civil war," I said.

"What?"

"The Ohbertians versus the Martyites. I got fed up with everyone arguing and saying we'd picked the wrong team."

"And if that stopped, you'd be captain again," said Azzie thoughtfully.

"Possibly."

We left it at that because a wicket fell and Azzie went in to bat. I knew quite a lot of people playing in the trials. Bazza Woolf from Mudlarks and Olly Sheringham from Stoney-heath were playing on our side and Liam Katz was captain of the opposition.

Bazza told me he'd played two games for Wyckham. Like Henry and Sam he'd been looking around for a team to play for this year because Mudlarks weren't in the League. "Guess who's been asking if he can play for us?" he said.

"Dunno. Mark Ramprakash?"

"No. Marty Lear," said Bazza with a grin. I felt sick, although I'd been half expecting it. "I wonder what that means?" said Bazza. "Trouble at Glory Gardens is there?"

"You'd better ask Sam and Henry," I said.

"I will," said Bazza.

Azzie was the star of the trial. He scored 53 and took two slip catches. The thing about Azzie's batting is time. He always has tons of it. He's never hurried or jumpy or caught in two minds like the rest of us. When the bowler runs up to the wicket he'll rock slightly on to his front foot but apart from that he doesn't move a muscle until the ball leaves the bowler's hand. Then he's forward or back – no one judges the

90

length of a delivery more quickly.

I didn't have a bad game either. I came in at the end of a big stand between Azzie and Olly Sheringham and scored a quick 20 before I was caught at extra cover. Then I took three wickets including a peach which bowled Liam Katz. Didn't he look sick? We won easily.

But I didn't come away from the game feeling particularly happy. I just couldn't stop thinking about Marty. He was too good a cricketer for Glory Gardens to lose. And anyway, we'd been friends for ages – I didn't want him to leave and play for Wyckham of all teams.

Marty's not the easiest person to have as a friend. He's moody and gloomy and always looking on the down side of things. But he's got a lot of good points, too. You can always count on him when you need help and he's incredibly generous, too. And, most important of all . . . he's the best bowler in the League.

On Saturday evening I was at home still thinking about Marty when Cal came round.

"It's working a treat," he said. "You wouldn't believe how fed up people are getting with Ohbert. I think there's going to be a mutiny. Jacky keeps going on about only bowling three overs on Wednesday and you'll never guess what?"

"Ohbert's picked my sister to play in the next game?"

"No, much stranger. Clive turned up to Nets."

"And Marty?"

"No. He's still sulking. But he'll come round. Clive didn't say much but he wants to get back in the team all right."

I told Cal the story of Marty's treason and all about the Colts trial and Azzie's 50.

"I can't believe Marty would play for Wyckham," said Cal finally. "They've always been the deadly enemy."

"You know how Marty gets," I said. "He's hardly said a word to anyone at school. He's not thinking straight."

"But playing for Wyckham!" said Cal in a low voice, as if he couldn't imagine anyone sinking so far.

"Who's picked for Wednesday?" I asked.

"Clive and Sam are in. Henry's out and Mack can't play for two weeks because his family's going on holiday. Oh, and they've picked you, in case you were wondering."

There was a muffled knock at the door and when I opened it I was surprised to see that it had started raining. There stood a very wet Ohbert.

"Oh but, Hooker. Can I come in?"

Ohbert dripped through the house and up to my room.

"Come to talk tactics for Wednesday, Ohbert?" said Cal.

"Er but, no but," said Ohbert. "I . . . I've . . . I want to stop being captain. And I don't care if that means I can't play. Though, of course . . ." Ohbert stopped in mid-sentence and looked around for help.

"First the mutiny. Now the captain's abandoning ship," said Cal.

"Why do you want to resign, Ohbert?" I said.

"Er well, I've changed my mind."

"Good. I hope it works better than the last one," said Cal.

Ohbert sat all scrunched up and wet. He looked at Cal, then at me. Finally he blurted, "And because you should be captain, Hooker."

"Too right," said Cal.

I was beginning to feel very guilty about putting poor old Ohbert through all this. "I thought you did a great job in the last game," I said.

"Oh thanks, Hooker," said Ohbert. "But I think one game being captain is enough, really."

"It'll go down in history," said Cal.

"What do we do now?" I asked.

"'Spose we'll have to have another election," said Cal.

As it turned out we didn't. The next week was half-term and the rain didn't stop. It rained all day Monday and Tuesday. On Wednesday morning Kiddo rang me to say that the Priory pitch was waterlogged and the Brass Castle game had been put off till Friday.

Once everyone got to hear about Ohbert's resignation, Azzie said I should be captain again and no one argued with him, not even Jacky. Jo said it was all right for me to be captain without an election if it was unanimous.

The next thing was to get Marty back in the team but no one saw him all week. When I went round to his house on Wednesday his mother told me he had gone off to play cricket. Oh no, I thought, it's too late. He's gone and joined Wyckham.

It was dry on Thursday – then it poured on Friday and all weekend. The Brass Castle game was cancelled and so was Nets.

It had been the worst half-term I could remember. And, of course, the sun was shining on Monday morning when we arrived back at school.

"Terrible news," said Jo rushing over when she saw me. "Wyckham and Croyland have gone top of the League."

She showed me the results.

Wyckham Wanderers *beat* Stoneyheath by 5 wickets
Croyland Crusaders *beat* Waterville by 18 runs
Glory Gardens v Brass Castle – rained off
Arctics v Old Courtiers – rained off

	PLAYED	WON	LOST	TIED	POINTS
Croyland	5	4	1		40
Wyckham	5	4	1		40
Glory Gardens	4	3	0	1	37*
Old Courtiers	4	2	1	1	27*
Stoneyheath	5	2	3		20
Arctics	4	1	3		12*
Brass Castle	4	1	3		12*
Waterville	5	0	5		0

* 2 points for cancelled game

"How did they manage to play last week?" I asked Jo.

"Perhaps they all flew to the south of France," said Frankie who had joined us to look at the results.

"Croyland and Wyckham have got artificial pitches," said Jo. "And they played on Thursday which was the only dry day last week."

Azzie saw us and came over. "Have you heard the bad news?" he said.

"Yeah," said Frankie. "Wyckham have been playing in their water wings and we're third."

"Worse than that," said Azzie. "Marty took four wickets for them."

Chapter Twelve

We set off for the match against Croyland Crusaders with the same team that Ohbert, Jacky and Jo had picked for the rained-off game against Brass Castle. To tell the truth, with Mack still on holiday, we didn't have much choice – particularly as Jo and I were determined to have Ohbert in the side ahead of Henry.

(in batting order)

Matthew Rose	Sam Keeping
Cal Sebastien	Frankie Allen
Azzie Nazar	Tylan Vellacott
Clive da Costa	Jacky Gunn
Erica Davies	Ohbert Bennett
Hooker Knight	12th man: Henry Rossi

Marty had kept out of our way at school all week although he couldn't avoid us in lessons. I didn't speak to him, but Frankie did.

"I told Marty I'd smash him all over the ground if he plays for Wyckham against us," he said.

"I bet he was petrified," said Cal. "What did he say?"

"Nothing. He's even gloomier than usual – if that's possible. He looks as if he thinks things will get a lot worse before they get worse."

"Well, it's his own fault; he's a traitor," said Jo. "You shouldn't talk to him."

Everyone was really desperate to win against Wyckham,

particularly if Marty played. But first we had to remember that Crusaders were the team to beat. They'd already given Wyckham a hiding and Kiddo reckons they are the toughest team in the League. If we didn't beat them our League challenge was as good as finished.

Crusaders ground is smaller than the Priory but the pitch looked brilliant on Wednesday evening. The outfield was in really good condition, especially after all the rain.

I lost the toss and their captain, Fred Duffield, put us in.

"Bet you a pound to nine pence it takes spin, kiddo," said Kiddo who'd played lots of times on the Crusaders ground. "Always does. Specially at the top end. And watch out for Jim Davy, their umpire. He's a strange old codger – got a queer sense of humour. He once tried to trip me up with his shooting stick when I was bowling. Nearly broke my leg."

Matthew faced up to the first ball of the match.

"Twenty overs apiece and may the best team win," said Jim Davy in a deep voice. He was a big, red-faced man and he sat firmly on his shooting stick behind the stumps at the bowler's end. He had a strange sort of accent, too, which made him sound a bit like an old-fashioned pirate. "Play," he boomed.

Fred, the Crusaders' captain opened the bowling. He took an enormous run up but I noticed he almost stopped in his delivery stride and all the speed came from his shoulder action. All the same, he was quite quick. Matthew left every ball in his first over. Most of them were short and outside the off-stump.

It wasn't long before Frankie was having his usual moan about Matthew's slow play. "Always the same. Just sits there and sets like a jelly."

"Five for 0 after four overs," said Jo.

"It's so exciting," said Frankie with a yawn. "I haven't had so much fun since I watched Geoff Boycott score a hundred on video."

Fred Duffield took himself out and brought on his spinner. Straight away both Cal and Matt were playing and missing.

Cal whacked one unconvincingly over square-leg for two. Then he was clean bowled going for another leg side swing.

Matthew played out another maiden, getting a groan a ball from Frankie and Clive, and then Azzie faced the spinner.

No one plays spin bowling better than Azzie. He uses his feet to get to the pitch of the ball and he has time to adjust his shot when he plays off the back foot. After his fifty in the Colts game Azzie had all his confidence back. He went straight on the attack, placing an on-drive between the bowler and mid-on.

At the half way stage we'd got 26 on the board. Azzie 13; Matthew 3.

"My word," said Frankie, doing his Richie Benaud impersonation. "Azzie Nazar is beginning to pose a few problems for the fielding side. Absolutely marvellous!"

Sam was the only one to laugh. He tried to answer him in a Geoff Boycott voice, "Cricket's all about posing problems, Richie," he said, only he sounded more like Jacky than Geoff Boycott.

Once Frankie starts, only Jo can switch him off and she was busy in the scorer's hut. So the Benaud commentary droned on and on. "Oh dear me. The bowler . . . what's his name? . . . ah yes, Friar, Friar is in his last over and Rose is still playing every ball defensively. Friar is bowling intelligently enough, pitching-up on the off-stump but, my word, Rose should be tucking away a few more singles. The run rate is still well under that magic five an over."

Azzie was making every effort to push the score along – a fierce pull went for four and then he played this classical forcing shot off the back foot through extra cover.

But Matthew kept getting the strike. He was trying to push the singles but the ball wasn't running for him. He survived a big appeal for a stumping. The keeper couldn't believe he wasn't out. Old Jim Davy shouted across to him, "Sorry old chap, I wasn't watching properly. I was thinking about my tea."

Azzie plays back with his back foot parallel to the stumps but his weight is still slightly forwards. The shot is controlled by the top hand and the high left elbow, power comes from the right hand. Notice how his back leg is braced and he pushes forward into the shot from his back leg.

In the fourteenth over, Azzie went for a quick single and Matt sent him back – but his call was late.

"Oh my word," said Frankie 'Benaud', "I fear there's a mix up here. Nazar is going to be run out. Yes, oh dear he fails to make his ground. My word, what a terrible way to get out. Mind you, he's scored a fine 24 out of a total of 40."

Clive jumped up determinedly and strolled out to the middle. But four balls later he was on his way back, given out lbw. The red-faced umpire grinned at him down the wicket and pointed a chubby finger. "Out, old chum," he said.

"Oh dear me," said Frankie. "There's a bit of a question mark about that. I think the action replay could show . . . was there a hint of an inside edge?"

No question as far as Clive was concerned. He stormed back to the pavilion, scowling back at old Jim from time to time. As he passed us he threw down his bat. "Lbw off the middle of the bat. I don't believe it. Blind and deaf old geezer shouldn't be umpiring cricket matches." He was so angry I wouldn't have been surprised if he had thrown his bat at the umpire.

"As I thought," said Frankie. "The batsman doesn't seem to be one hundred per cent in agreement with that decision. But if the finger goes up you're out – and there's no arguing with that."

There were only five overs to go and we needed at least 30 more runs to make a game of it. "Tell Matthew to hit out or get out," I said to Erica as she put on her gloves and set off for the middle.

At least Matthew did as he was told; he hit an edgy two over the bowler's head and was caught next ball at mid-off.

"My word, eight runs off fifteen overs. That's really not quite good enough." That was Frankie's commentary on Matthew's innings – and, for once, I had to agree with him.

I walked out to join Erica thinking, all we can do now is slog and hope to hit as many runs as possible. But that wasn't easy because Fred Duffield had come back on at the bottom end and he was bowling fast.

I missed my first ball, edged the next over the keeper's diving right hand for two, hit another two through the covers and then played all round a yorker and was clean bowled.

Sam was run out at the bowler's end going for a quick single and Frankie went in to bat – much to everyone's relief because it brought an end to the running commentary. His first ball was short and fast and he played an astonishing hook off his nose. The ball went off the bat like a rocket and disappeared miles over a hedge into a garden at the bottom end of the ground. It bounced high in the air and – CRASH. It sounded like glass.

"Splendid shot, boy," boomed Jim Davy, signalling a six with his arms raised high.

Seconds later a very angry gardener appeared holding our cricket ball. "You vandals. That went straight through my greenhouse," he cried.

"Ah, well done, you've found the ball, matey," said old Jim Davy, completely ignoring the man's complaint. The gardener went bright red with rage. He disappeared back into his garden still holding the cricket ball and shouting about calling the police and sending us the bill.

"Oh dear, I hope it wasn't something I said," old Jim said as he sent for a replacement ball. After a short delay Kiddo found one and the game continued. I noticed Kiddo disappearing through the hedge to have a word with the gardener – just as well, we didn't want the game interrupted by a police raid.

But if Frankie had had his way there'd have been another hole in the greenhouse. He went for a second huge hit in the same direction, but this time he got bowled all ends up.

"Just as well or we'd have run out of balls," laughed Jim Davy.

Frankie swaggered back towards us. "My word, what a fine blow," he said. "Straight in the tomatoes."

"If you don't go and say sorry to that man you'll probably get arrested," said Jo.

Erica and Tylan scored well at the death – 18 runs came off the last 15 balls, including a lovely pulled four by Erica. We finished on 78 – and that was fairly amazing after our slow start.

"I just knew Tylan would play well today," said Frankie. "He's got his lucky smelly socks on."

"They're all smelly," said Azzie. "How do you know which are the lucky ones?"

"Instinct," said Frankie with a laugh.

At the end of the innings old Jim the umpire had a word with Clive. "Sorry, old chap," he said. "I think, on second thoughts you may have got a nick on that one. Still, only a game isn't it?"

I'm not sure that Clive entirely agreed. His eyes opened wide but he didn't reply.

HOME TEAM CROYLAND CRUS.	V GLORY GARDENS	AWAY TEAM	AT CROYLAND. DATE JUN.E.8TH.

INNINGS OF GLORY GARDENS...... | TOSS WON BY C.C. WEATHER SUNNY

BATSMAN	RUNS SCORED	HOW OUT	BOWLER	SCORE
1 M. ROSE	1.1.1.1.1.2 ≫	ct BUNKER	DUFFIELD	8
2 C. SEBASTIEN	2.1.1.2 ≫	bowled	FRIAR	6
3 A. NAZAR	2.2.1.1.4.2.1.4.2.3.2 ≫	RUN	OUT	24
4 C. DA COSTA	1 ≫	l bw	MARRIOTT	1
5 E. DAVIES	1.1.2.1.1.2.11.4.4.1	NOT	OUT	15
6 H. KNIGHT	2.2 ≫	bowled	DUFFIELD	4
7 S. KEEPING	2. ≫	RUN	OUT	2
8 F. ALLEN	6 ≫	bowled	DUFFIELD	6
9 T. VELLACOTT	1.1.1	NOT	OUT	3
10				
11				

FALL OF WICKETS													
	1	2	3	4	5	6	7	8	9	10	BYES	2.1	4	TOTAL EXTRAS 9
SCORE	7	40	41	45	49	64	60				L.BYES 1.	1	TOTAL 78
BAT NO	2	3	4	1	6	7	8				WIDES 1.1.1	3	FOR
											NO BALLS 1	1	WKTS 7

SCORE AT A GLANCE

BOWLING ANALYSIS ⊙ NO BALL + WIDE

BOWLER	1	2	3	4	5	6	7	8	9	10	11	12	13	OVS	MDS	RUNS	WKT
1 F. DUFFIELD	M	::1	X	2N· 6W· 2.2N· +2										4	1	19	3
2 I. JARVIS	·.2	·.·.	M	1··	X									4	1	5	0
3 D. FRIAR	·.·. 2w.	·.2 ·.21	·.·. ·.4.	M	X									4	1	11	1
4 N. HAMMOND	·.2 ·.1	4·· 2··	·.1 2·1	X										3	0	14	0
5 C. MARRIOTT	·.·. 13·	W +·.+1 ·.1 2··	+1 ·1 121											4	0	16	1
6 S. BALDWIN	·⊙1 4·1													1	0	8	0
7																	
8																	
9																	

102

Chapter Thirteen

" I 'd get the spinners on early, if I were you," said Kiddo. "It's turning like a banana – and there's nothing like a couple of early wickets to slow down the scoring."

Kiddo hadn't said a word to me about Ohbert's short spell as captain. That's one of the good things about him – he doesn't interfere. He lets us get on with running the team the way we want. On the other hand we do have to listen to an awful lot of tactical talk from him. He's full of theories and stories about the 'golden days' when he played county cricket.

"Pressure, kiddoes," he said. "That's what it's all about. Put them under pressure and you've got them where you want them."

"Would it help if Frankie sat on one of them?" said Tylan.

Kiddo pretended not to hear. "If you try to keep the weaker batsman on strike and bowl to your field, you're half way there. If they're under pressure, they'll start to take chances and that's when the wickets fall."

It isn't that Kiddo doesn't talk a lot of sense about cricket – he's taught us loads. The problem is he doesn't know when to stop and we have to sort out the good stuff from the boring bits. I wasn't too sure about opening with both spinners. Sometimes Tylan can give a lot of runs away and we didn't have a big score to defend – especially on a small pitch with a fast outfield. So I bowled Jacky from the top end and Cal at the other.

The Crusaders' openers came out with the umpires. One of

the batsmen was wearing a helmet and an arm guard. Old Jim Davy cracked him over the head with his shooting stick. "They seem to work all right," he said with a laugh.

"Has anyone told him Cal's bowling?" said Frankie staring at the helmetted batsman. "The only protection you need against Cal is an alarm clock to keep you awake."

"Just make sure *you* stay awake, fat man," said Cal. "Remember you're fielding today, not snoozing behind the stumps as you usually do."

Sam was keeping wicket and chuckling away at Frankie's jokes as ever. Frankie only had to open his mouth and Sam fell about laughing. Perhaps it wasn't a good idea to have Frankie next to him in the slips, but he's a good slip fielder and he's not a lot of use anywhere else.

The Crusaders got off to a flier. It wasn't really our fault, they just rode their luck and the runs rattled along. The batsman with the helmet got two streaky edges along the ground through slips in the first over and Frankie had to chase all the way to the boundary. The outfield was getting faster and faster as it dried in the sun.

Then both batsmen really went for Cal. He was pulled for four and twice driven through the covers. After three overs they'd scored 21 and I had to take Frankie out of the slips and put him on the mid-wicket boundary. I moved Clive deeper at extra-cover and Matthew out to the long-on boundary, too.

Cal bowled three balls on a length which had the batsman with the helmet playing forward defensively. Then he bowled a short one, a terrible long hop. The non-striker was half way down the wicket, ready to run if the ball got clouted into the outfield as it deserved to be. The batsman waited with his bat raised. Then he took a huge swing and gave a cry of anguish as he missed it. He turned to watch the ball bounce a second time and lob gently into his wicket. He took off his helmet, smacked his bat against his pad and walked slowly back to the pavilion shaking his head.

"That's what I call pressure bowling," shouted Frankie

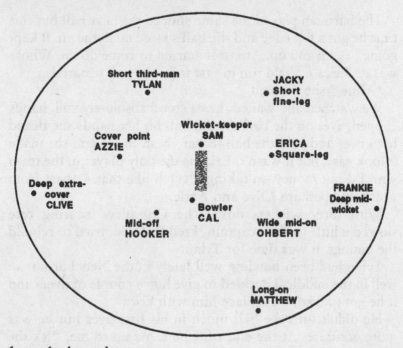

Short third-man
TYLAN

JACKY
Short
fine-leg

Wicket-keeper
SAM

Cover point
AZZIE

ERICA
Square-leg

Deep extra-
cover
CLIVE

FRANKIE
Deep mid-
wicket

Bowler
CAL

Mid-off
HOOKER

Wide mid-on
OHBERT

Long-on
MATTHEW

from the boundary.

Cal bowed and then threw a high catch to Frankie which
he dropped. "Try catching it with your mouth," said Cal.

Jacky was now bowling with a lot of control but the opener
was still going for his shots. Finally, he played a cross-bat shot
outside the off-stump and edged it to Sam who took a brilliant catch. I don't know how he got a glove on it because he
was standing right up to Jacky, but the ball smacked into his
gloves off the bottom edge.

"Sam the man!" chanted Frankie from the boundary and
half the team rushed over to the keeper to congratulate him.

I brought the field in for the new batsman who tried to
follow on where the openers had left off. He swung a four
past the diving Frankie at mid-wicket. Cal wasn't pleased.

"Get your body behind it. There's enough of it," he said.

Frankie, puffing back from the boundary with the ball,
stuck his tongue out.

105

The batsman played the same shot to the next ball but this time he got a top edge and the ball soared up in the air. It kept going . . . up and up. At last it started to come down. Whose was it? Erica's. She'd run in fast from deepish square-leg.

"Mine," she shouted.

We watched and waited. Erica stood absolutely still, hands cupped, eyes on the ball. As the ball hit her hands she flexed her knees and held the ball to her chest. In the end she made it look easy, but it wasn't. Erica is the only player in the team who I'd put money on taking a catch like that – apart from Mack and perhaps Clive and Azzie.

With three wickets down the Crusaders' scoring rate slowed a little as their captain, Fred Duffield, tried to rebuild the innings. It was time for Tylan.

Tylan had been bowling well lately in the Nets but not so well in the middle. I decided to give him a couple of overs and if he got tonked, I'd replace him with Erica.

He didn't turn the ball much in his first over but he was quite accurate. At the end of it he came up to me. "It's the wrong end," he said. "Can I bowl up the hill instead?"

I'd been thinking that, too. I'd realised my mistake after the first ball of Tylan's over. Kiddo was right, the ball didn't turn so much at the bottom end.

I brought Erica on to switch ends for Tylan. She immediately found her line and length and with her last ball she got one to nip back between bat and pad and clip the off-bail. That was tough on Tylan – I could hardly take Erica off after she'd taken a wicket.

I bowled at the top and slowly we started to get back into the game. From the ninth to the thirteenth over they put on only eight runs. The fielding was tight apart from Frankie who was being followed around by the ball. Wherever I put him the batsmen hit it to him. He was red as a tomato from running and green from sliding along the boundary – it didn't help matters that he wasn't wearing spikes. He slipped over again trying to intercept a drive and let it through for two.

"Tell them to stop making me run about," he sighed to me. "I'm so hot you could fry an egg on my head." He looked dangerously overheated; his shirt was sticking to his body and he was breathing like a steam train.

With seven overs to go the Crusaders still needed 31 runs to win. But they had plenty of wickets in hand. So I decided to risk Tylan again to see if he could pick up a wicket.

He started with a wide down the leg side, then Fred Duffield drove him for a couple of twos, but Tylan struck back at the end of the over, picking up a smart caught and bowled off a leading edge.

Fred Duffield hit the first ball of my next over straight to Ohbert at square-leg. It was really a dolly to anyone else, but Ohbert didn't even manage to get a hand on it. It bounced off his chest and as he turned round to look for the ball the Crusaders ran a single.

There was a huge groan from the other fielders, especially Clive, and Ohbert looked miserable. I went over to him.

"Don't let it worry you, Ohbert," I said. "I dropped four against Stoneyheath – you've got a long way to go to catch up with me."

"Oh but, Hooker," said Ohbert. "I'm not as bad as that. Everyone knows you can't catch."

I didn't know what to say to that – so I just slapped Ohbert on the back. He started coughing and spluttering and I walked away.

Tylan was now getting the ball to turn a lot and he had the new batsman playing and missing three times outside the off-stump. Sam appealed loudly for a stumping off the third one but the batsman had kept his toe just behind the line.

"Now that was close," said Jim Davy, "but I think I'll have to give the batsman the benefit of the doubt."

With four overs remaining they still needed 23 runs.

Fred, the captain, decided to chance his arm. He swung a well-pitched-up ball from me away on the off-side for two. I pushed the field out on the boundary. He missed with two more wild swings and finally hit one out towards Frankie at deep extra-cover. Frankie bent down to stop it, got in a tangle and let the ball trickle through his legs for four.

"What a plum!" said Cal under his breath.

"Can't you get your body behind it, blubberguts?" yelled Clive.

Frankie walked in with the ball and lobbed it to me. "If he says that again, I'll job him one," he said staring at Clive. I got the feeling he was only half joking which wasn't like Frankie at all. He turned to walk back to his fielding position, red-faced and mumbling to himself, "It hit a bump – any fool could see that."

Tylan kept Fred Duffield away from the strike for three balls. Then they ran a leg-bye and Fred hit him over the top for four.

That left one ball of Tylan's spell. Fred charged down the wicket to meet it but didn't quite get to the pitch. The ball took a thick outside edge and flew on the bounce to Ohbert at fly slip. Fred must have spotted it was Ohbert and thought there was an easy single in it but before he'd taken a stride Ohbert stuck out his hand and caught the ball cleanly. To tell the truth it had come so quickly, he could have hardly seen it. Fred turned and slipped. Ohbert stood still looking at the ball in his hand.

"Throw it, Ohbert. Throw it, you fool," yelled Cal.

Ohbert woke up and underarmed the ball gently to Sam who had the bails off just before Fred made his ground.

"Afraid you've got to go this time, old chap," said old Jim Davy, raising his finger.

"So cool," said Sam grinning at Ohbert. "So casual!"

"Let's hear it for the incredible Ohbert," shouted Frankie from the boundary. It hadn't taken him long to get over his tantrum. Sam laughed and said, "Three cheers for Ohbert."

Ohbert just grinned and looked silly.

Two overs left. I could bowl Erica at the top end but who should I bring on for the last over? I'd got in a bit of a mess with bringing back Tylan and now I'd run out of bowlers. There was only one thing for it. It had to be Clive.

Erica's over went for only four runs – just what we needed.

They wanted seven off the last over. I set the field back with five on the leg side and four on the off.

"Bowl middle stump and we win," I said to Clive.

"Trust me," said Clive. I wasn't worried about Clive being nervous; over-confidence was more likely to be his problem.

His first ball was a real loosener down the leg side and it would have gone for four runs if Cal hadn't brought off a diving, sliding stop on the square-leg boundary. The next ball was a beaut; it bounced a bit more and went over the swinging bat and only just over middle stump. They scampered a quick single off the third ball of the over. Four to win. The next delivery cannoned into the pads and Clive screamed for lbw. "Not out," boomed Jim Davy. "But close," he added.

There was nearly a run out next ball. The striker dropped the ball down in front of him and called for a single. "No!" screamed his partner seeing Clive following up fast. The batsman turned and just got his bat down as Clive hit the stumps with his underarm throw.

So it came down to four needed off the last ball. Out went the field again. This time everyone was on the boundary. I went to 'cow corner' – between Matthew at long-on and Frankie at deep mid-wicket. The ball was on middle stump but the batsman swung with all his strength and connected. It sped out to the mid-wicket boundary between Frankie and me. No, it was much closer to Frankie. Was it going to beat him to the boundary? Not quite. Frankie was nearly in line with the ball. Would he let it through his legs again? I kept running towards him and I was about five yards away when he picked up on the run with both hands and threw in hard to Clive at the bowler's end.

"Here's one from blubberguts," he shouted as the ball smacked into Clive's hands right over the stumps. We'd won by two runs.

109

Frankie picks up on the run. Notice how he gets both hands on the ball and his foot is behind it as a second line of defence.

Cal rushed up to Frankie. "Brilliant, but how did you manage to bend down like that?" he said slapping him on the shoulder.

Frankie yelped, "Ouch! Bang on my BCG," he cried. "That's all I need. Get me a bucket of water."

Azzie got Player of the Match but the cap was a bit wrecked because Gatting had got into our changing room. He'd found a bag of toffees in Frankie's kit and eaten them all. He must have had the cap for afters.

"He's eaten my French homework, too," said Frankie, hunting through his bag for one remaining toffee.

"I don't believe it," said Cal.

"Nor do I," grinned Frankie. "But perhaps Kiddo will."

It had been a great game. Perhaps we might have won more easily if our fielding had been tighter. Without Frankie and Ohbert Glory Gardens would probably be a better team, but it wouldn't be half so much fun.

HOME TEAM	CROYLAND CRUS.	v	GLORY GARDENS	AWAY TEAM	AT CROYLAND	DATE JUNE 8TH

INNINGS OF CROYLAND CRUSADERS... | TOSS WON BY C.C... WEATHER SUNNY.

BATSMAN	RUNS SCORED	HOW OUT	BOWLER	SCORE
1 C. MARRIOTT	2·3·4·2·1 ⟫	bowled	SEBASTIEN	12
2 S. BALDWIN	3·2·1·2 ⟫	ct KEEPING	GUNN	8
3 F. DUFFIELD	1·1·1·1·2·1·2·2·2·1·2·2·4·4 ⟫	RUN	OUT	27
4 N. ARMSTRONG	4 ⟫	ct DAVIES	SEBASTIEN	4
5 M. DEENOO	1·1 ⟫	bowled	DAVIES	2
6 I. JARVIS	1·1·2 ⟫	c & b	VELLACOTT	4
7 N. BUNKER	1·1·1·1·1	NOT	OUT	5
8 D. FRIAR	1·1·2·1	NOT	OUT	5
9				
10				
11				

FALL OF WICKETS

SCORE	21	25	30	38	51	68	7	8	9	10
BAT NO	1	2	4	5	6	3				

BYES	————————
L.BYES	1·1·1·1·1·1·1 = 7
WIDES	1·1 = 2
NO BALLS	

TOTAL EXTRAS	9
TOTAL	76
FOR WKTS	6

SCORE AT A GLANCE

BOWLING ANALYSIS ⊙ NO BALL + WIDE

BOWLER	1	2	3	4	5	6	7	8	9	10	11	12	13	OVS	MDS	RUNS	WKT
1 J. GUNN	·2· 3··	·2· ·-11	·1· 2W.	·1· ···	X									4	0	14	1
2 C. SEBASTIEN	·4· 3·2	··· W·1	1·4W ·1·	·1· ·1	X									4	0	18	2
3 T. VELLACOTT	··2 ···	X	4·2 2·4·	··· ·12·4·	X									4	0	14	1
4 E. DAVIES	W ··2	X	·1· ·1											3	1	7	1
5 H. KNIGHT	·1· ·1	·2· ··	1·· ··	·12 ·4	X									4	0	12	0
6 C. DA COSTA	2· ·1													1	0	4	0
7																	
8																	
9																	

Chapter Fourteen

Next day at school I spoke to Marty for the first time in more than two weeks. Marty had hardly said a word to anyone, particularly since he had started playing for the Wanderers. Even when Frankie called him 'a traitor and a trundler' he just walked away without saying a thing.

I can't remember which of us spoke first but I know he asked how we'd got on against Croyland.

"Beat them by two runs," I said.

"Oh brilliant," said Marty, seeming to forget for a moment that he wasn't a Glory Gardens player anymore.

"And did Wyckham win?" I asked.

"Er . . . yes," said Marty. I looked at him and he must have known I was about to ask the obvious question, "I got three for 12, if you must know."

"Well, I'm glad you're having fun," I said.

Marty looked at me steadily. "I'm not, much," he said.

"Then why . . ." I began.

"All right," said Marty, "I do play cricket for fun. But there's more to it than that. I want to win. And I want to play for a team that takes winning seriously."

"And we don't, I suppose. Perhaps you've forgotten that, unlike Wyckham, we haven't lost a single game yet."

"I still say it's not serious when you pick people like Ohbert and even Frankie before Sam and Henry," he said.

"Even if we still win?"

"Even if you still win."

"But you know Henry and Sam aren't really Glory Gardens players." And I should have said, You aren't a real Wyckham player either.

"Why not?"

"Because sooner or later they'll be playing for Mudlarks again – because that's their team."

"Well, I don't suppose anyone would have me back anyway," said Marty gloomily.

"I would."

He looked at me for a moment as if he was going to accept my offer, then he said, "It's too late. I've already promised I'll play for Wyckham."

"Against us?"

"Yeah."

"Then you're in for the biggest hiding you've ever known," I said angrily.

"We'll see," said Marty slowly, and he walked away.

———— • ————

When the news got out that Marty was playing against us everyone turned on him. Jacky said he'd never speak to him again; Frankie blacked him out of the team photo on the wall of the pavilion and even Cal and Azzie, who were Marty's closest friends, said they were finished with him.

At Nets on Saturday we saw the full list of last week's results. There was now no doubt about it – the Wyckham game was the crunch.

Waterville *lost to* Old Courtiers by 4 wickets
Stoneyheath & Stockton *beat* Arctics by 17 runs
Croyland Crusaders *lost to* Glory Gardens by 2 runs
Brass Castle *lost to* Wyckham Wanderers by 20 runs

	PLAYED	WON	LOST	TIED	PTS
Wyckham	6	5	1		50
Glory Gardens	5	4		1	47*
Croyland	6	4	2		40
Old Courtiers	5	3	1	1	37*
Stoneyheath	6	3	3		30
Arctics	5	1	4		12*
Brass Castle	5	1	4		12*
Waterville	6	0	6		0

* 2 points for cancelled game

"Easy peasy," said Frankie. "Beat Marty and the Wanderers. Win the League."

"Wouldn't it be nice if everyone in the world had such a simple view of life?" said Cal.

"It would be horrible," said Jo. "No-one would wash, the world would be littered with old rubbish and everyone would slob about eating junk food and making stupid, unfunny jokes."

"Sounds great to me," said Frankie.

"Imagine having to face Marty if they win," said Jacky.

"And Liam Katz. I can hear him crowing now," said Azzie.

"Katz don't crow," said Tylan.

"They're not going to win," said Jo. "Don't even think about it. And get out there and practise until you drop."

"Oh, I don't know why we bother. What's the point of net practice?" moaned Clive.

"I'll tell you if you like," said Kiddo from the other side of the pavilion.

"Oh no!" whispered Frankie. "I didn't know *he* was listening."

"For a start," Kiddo began, "practising allows you to experiment. Take young Calvin, for instance. If he tries something like a top spinner in a match and it doesn't work, he won't try it again. In practice you can keep doing it until you get it right. And in the end that makes you a more exciting player – less ordinary. Does that make sense?"

"Have you got that, Ohbert?" asked Frankie.

"Oh but, what?" said Ohbert coming out from under his Walkman.

"Mr Johnstone wants you to be more exciting and less ordinary," said Frankie.

"Oh but, I'll try, Frankie," said Ohbert.

Kiddo continued. "But that doesn't mean a bowler should mix it up all the time. That's Tylan's trouble. He wants to bowl googlies and flippers before he can bowl six straight leg breaks in a row. So practice is about doing the same thing until you've got it perfect. Take batting, for instance. At Nets you've got a chance to get into a groove. You can play 50 cuts in a row or 50 off-drives. That gives you a chance to polish your technique." He took a deep breath, "Does that answer your questions, Clive?"

"Yes it does, doesn't it, Clive?" said Frankie before Clive could answer. "Good, I'm glad that's settled then," he added and rushed off to get changed in case Kiddo was going to say any more.

You could see that everyone, even Clive, was working extra hard in practice. The shadow of Marty and Wyckham Wanderers was hanging over the whole team.

Dave Wing talked to the bowlers about concentration. He got us bowling at a mark on the pitch. "Keep your eye on it when you release the ball and think only about hitting that spot every time," he said.

The point we aimed at was further up for the slow bowlers and slightly shorter for the fast bowlers, like this:

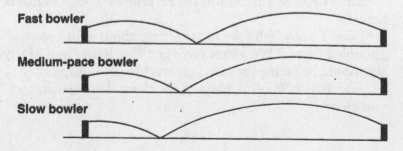

Fast bowler

Medium-pace bowler

Slow bowler

Kiddo showed the batting group how to play spin bowling. "The main thing to remember," he said, "is not to make your mind up before the ball is bowled. Play it on its merit. If it's turning and you can get to the pitch, play forward and smother the spin. But don't just lunge. If it's short, go back and play the spin off the pitch. Watch the ball and play it late."

He showed us how to keep balanced and to play the ball with a soft grip on the handle, so if we got an edge it probably wouldn't carry to the fielder.

"Can you tell which way the ball's going to turn when the bowler bowls it?" asked Erica.

"They usually give you a clue," said Kiddo. "I always watch a spinner's shoulders. Look at Calvin and Tylan when they bowl, for example."

"But that's not the end of the story," said Kiddo. "Sometimes the bowler himself doesn't know which way it will turn. Sometimes he'll deliberately not spin the ball to fool you. So, in the end, you should play it on length and off the pitch."

"Do you play different attacking shots to spinners?" asked Matthew.

"*You* don't play attacking shots to anyone," said Frankie.

"Not really," said Kiddo to Matthew. "If it's short you can cut or pull; if it's a half-volley you drive. The only extra shot is the sweep which you can play to a well-pitched-up ball on or outside the leg stump."

"And Frankie's reverse sweep?" said Azzie.

"I've got nothing against it, kiddo – except it's a high risk shot unless you practise and practise before playing it in a game," said Kiddo.

"Unless you're a natural-born reverse sweeper," muttered Frankie.

"I don't know why we're worrying about spin bowlers," grumbled Clive. "Wyckham have got Win Reifer and Marty. We should be facing the bowling machine at full speed."

"And Bazza Woolf is playing for them. He's quick, too," said Henry.

116

"You haven't forgotten that their spinner took four for 8 against us last year," said Azzie. "And Liam Katz is bowling spin this year, too."

"Is there nothing SuperKatz can't do?" sighed Frankie.

That made five top class bowlers. But I had to agree with Clive for once. The one who worried me most was Marty –

Tylan dips his left shoulder as he bowls and his body pulls *away* in the same direction; the leg break ball spins towards the slips (for a right-hander).

Cal's right shoulder comes round and across the body. Notice how straight he keeps his left side. The off-break spins into you from off to leg.

he had a big point to prove.

After Nets it was time for the selection committee. I was expecting some arguments even though Jacky and Jo were the original Ohbertians, but we picked the side I wanted without any problems.

Matthew Rose	Frankie Allen
Cal Sebastien	Tylan Vellacott
Clive da Costa	Jacky Gunn
Azzie Nazar	Ohbert Bennett
Erica Davies	Reserves:
Hooker Knight	Henry Rossi
Mack McCurdy	Sam Keeping

It was the old Glory Gardens team without Marty. And, if we were going to show Marty, this was the team that had to do it.

I think Sam understood – though he was disappointed not to be picked. Henry sulked a bit and combed his hair a lot, but in the end he said, "I'll come along and watch you lose."

"Bet you as many hamburgers as you can eat that we win," said Frankie.

Chapter Fifteen

T he big day came – and it was hot. We sweated through the morning and afternoon at school thinking about nothing but the game. Marty was still trying to keep out of our way, but, unluckily for him, he kept bumping into Frankie and Frankie can't keep his mouth shut.

"What's the difference between Marty Lear and a squashed chicken in the road?" he asked Marty. Marty didn't reply. "Not much," continued Frankie, "except the chicken didn't get to the other side." Marty glared at him and walked off.

Just after maths Frankie cornered Marty again as he was rushing out of the classroom. "I hope you know they still hang people for treason," he said.

"So what?" grunted Marty.

"So we'll have a swinging time tonight."

"I should save your strength for the game, Frankie," said Marty. "You'll need it."

———————— • ————————

There was a big crowd sitting in the sun at the Priory Ground when we arrived. Azzie's dad was there and Clive's aunt and a lot of people from school including my sister. I don't know why she bothers because she hates cricket – I think she just comes to annoy me. Wyckham had brought along a load of supporters, too; they almost outnumbered the Glory Gardens fans.

I won the toss and decided to bat. I always like batting first at the Priory and I was pleased that Liam Katz looked disappointed when I told him.

Kiddo was walking round the ground with Gatting. He was looking as nervous as we were and he even forgot to come over and give us his usual pep talk.

Frankie made up for it. "Righto, kiddoes," he said. "Now pin back your ears. The big secret is that you've got to get more runs than they do. Remember that and you won't go far wrong. Now, I've got a last minute tip for each of you. Clive – keep your eye on the ball. Calvin – I want you to get a bagful of wickets. Hooker – you'll need an old head on young shoulders . . ." And so he went on and on but I stopped listening to him.

Marty opened the bowling with Win Reifer. There's not much to choose between them in terms of pace, but Marty's a lot more accurate. Our first 8 runs came off extras, mostly wides and no balls from Win. You never feel safe with Win though. He'll bowl three rubbish balls, then suddenly he'll send down an unplayable one. He nearly had Cal with a quick bouncer which Cal shaped to hook but the ball got too big on him and he gloved it just short of the keeper.

At the other end Marty was bowling beautifully. Neither Cal nor Matthew could lay a bat on him to begin with. He opened with a maiden, although Cal took a single off a leg-bye which was the closest thing to lbw I've ever seen. Marty appealed furiously and sank to his knees when the umpire said, "Not out." Then he missed Matthew's off-stump by a whisker.

In his second over he bowled Matthew with a brute of a ball and had Azzie dropped first ball in the slips by none other than Liam Katz.

"Good old SuperKatz. He's saved Azzie from a golden blob," cried Frankie, loud enough for Liam to hear. He scowled at us and Kiddo told Frankie to shut up.

Marty's next ball was very fast and short. Azzie stepped inside it and hooked it in the air, but safe, for four. Marty versus Azzie looked as if it would be the contest of the game. But no, it all ended next ball. Marty bowled a yorker. Azzie drove at it. The ball came off the toe of the bat, bounced up on to his pads and deflected gently into his stumps. Liam ran out of the slips and did a little dance round Marty. Then he looked in Frankie's direction and bowed sarcastically.

"Look at that performing monkey," said Frankie. "I'll show him when I get in."

"I hope things don't get that bad," said Mack.

But we all knew, Liam included, that Glory Gardens' best batsman had gone cheaply. The score was 12 for two.

I decided to try and steady things down. I'd already told Erica to pad up early in case we lost early wickets. Now I decided to send her in ahead of Clive to protect him from Marty. Clive protested, of course, but I took no notice. As Erica set off I said, "Calm it down for a couple of overs but keep the runs coming."

Cal managed to clip a couple of twos off Reifer and then Liam took Marty off and replaced him at the canal end with Bazza Woolf. He's keeping Marty back for a burst at Clive and me, I thought – probably just what I'd have done.

Erica spoke briefly to Cal and they started to push the singles about. Bazza was swinging it a bit and, although he's not as fast as Win, he was more difficult to get away.

Win Reifer came off – none for 16 – and Liam brought on Youz Mohamed, his spinner, from the Woodcock Lane end. That's the same end that Youz bowled from last year when he nearly demolished us with 4 for eight. I remembered him well – he can turn the ball both ways and he bowls a brilliant quicker ball which is really hard to pick. I remembered, too, that I got 26 not out in that game.

Cal watched the first two balls of spin carefully. It didn't seem to be turning that much.

"If only Cal can hold out for a bit longer . . ." I began and stopped mid sentence. There was a cheer and Cal's off-stump was leaning back at 45 degrees.

"Well he can't," said Frankie. "Your turn, Clive. Give 'em some stick."

Clive looked oddly out of sorts against the spinner and not much better against Bazza. He played and missed three times in a row and even when he connected he was scratching about – the ball just wasn't hitting the middle of his bat like it usually does. Clive hates being tied down and at last he swung in frustration at a ball on middle stump. It only just cleared mid-off's outstretched fingers and went for two streaky runs. At the half way stage, we had struggled to just 30 for three.

Erica started to use her feet against Youz's spin. She hit him twice through the off-side and the tactic seemed to be working because his bowling became less accurate and Clive was able to pull a slow long-hop for four. Liam immediately brought Marty back. With his first ball he trapped Erica lbw. She'd scored 12 vital runs.

I walked slowly to the wicket trying to remember all the things Kiddo had told me about concentrating before an innings. "Never mind how well a bowler is bowling," he'd once said. "Remember he'll stop feeling so confident if you start hitting the ball in the middle of the bat. Every time you push a single, it's one up to you." Old Kiddo can be a bit of a bore at times but he knows his cricket. And he badly wanted us to win the League. I knew that. There he was pacing round the boundary. He saw me looking at him and he gave me a wave and a thumbs up.

As I took guard I said to myself, don't give it away, for Kiddo's sake. I watched the first ball all the way from Marty's hand on to my bat. It was quick and short of a length but I glanced it off the middle down to long-leg for a single. Off the mark! That felt better.

Marty was now giving it everything. He beat Clive three times in a row outside the off-stump. The third ball was so quick that it beat the keeper, too, and we ran two byes. Marty was really worked up. He stood in the middle of the pitch with his hands on his hips and when the ball was thrown back to him he held it up to Clive. "It's red and round and you're supposed to hit it! Right?" And he stormed back to his bowling mark.

His next ball was short and fast. Clive leaned back and hooked hard. Marty followed through right down the pitch and batsman and bowler were almost side by side as they watched the ball disappear for six in the brambles to the right of the pavilion. "You know what it looks like," said Clive to Marty, "you go and find it."

Youz beat me completely with the first ball of his next over. It turned sharply and just missed the outside edge of my lunging forward defensive. Liam brought in a slip and a short point but the next ball was a full toss which I swung away for two.

I decided to try and play the spin off the pitch or use my feet and get down the wicket – just as Kiddo had told us. I dabbed a quicker ball through the slip area and got down to the other end. Watching Youz Mohamed close up I could see how much zip he put into spinning the ball. He almost bowled himself off his feet at times and he can turn the ball even more than Tylan. Clive was probably still a bit wound up after hitting the six and thinking about having another go at Marty. He came down the track to the last ball of the over but the spinner saw him coming and sent down a quick, flat delivery. Clive missed it and Charlie Gale, their keeper, had the bails off before he could turn around. It was an intelligent piece of cricket and Clive trudged back to the pavilion.

Marty had one over left and I decided that I'd try and play him out and then attack the last four overs. Mack joined me in the centre.

"What's Marty had for breakfast?" he said. "I've never seen him bowl so fast."

"He's just showing off," I said.

"How many runs do we need?" asked Mack.

"About 30 should do it."

"Okay, six an over. No problem."

Marty's first ball was a fast yorker on leg stump. I just got my bat down and the ball squirted to square-leg. Mack wanted a single but I sent him back. The next ball was short, outside off-stump and I cut hard but Liam Katz dived at point and cut off a certain four. The third was a beauty; it reared off the pitch. I just managed to get my bat and gloves out of the way of it and it flew past my nose. I heard it smack into the keeper's gloves. Three balls left.

Marty roared in and then bowled a slower ball. I picked it in time and forced it away on the off-side for two. I knew the next one would be quick, and it was. Marty hammered the ball into the pitch and I ducked. Stupidly I took my eye off it and there was a sudden stabbing pain in my elbow. The ball lobbed in the air and the keeper caught it, "Owzthat?"

"Not out," I said angrily rubbing my elbow. I was more angry with myself, though. The ball hadn't got up as much as I expected and I'd ducked into it.

Marty rushed up to me. "You okay, Hooker?" he said.

"Yeah," I grunted. "Course I am."

Old Sid looked at my elbow and told me to take my time before I faced the next ball. My arm felt numb and I couldn't grip the bat properly with my left hand but I didn't want to show Marty he'd hurt me. The pain made me concentrate even harder. Marty's last ball was a fuller length, outside off-stump and I dropped my wrists and late cut it off the middle of the bat. There was a sharp pain as I played the shot. "Yes," shouted Mack and we ran three.

That was the end of Marty. He'd taken three for 16.

"I'm going to try and give it some welly," I said to Mack. "Get your eye in for a couple of balls and then you have a go."

But it wasn't as simple as that. The new bowler bowled very straight and he wasn't easy to get away, particularly with Liam's tight defensive field and my sore elbow.

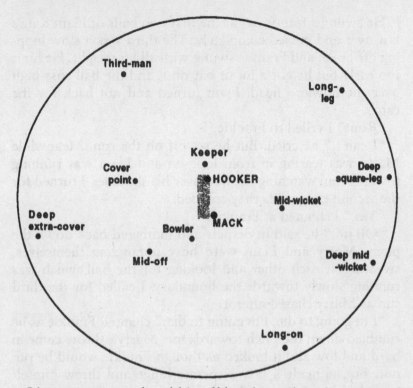

Liam came on to bowl his off-breaks at the other end and Mack cracked him for four past deep mid-wicket. But he paid for it two balls later when he missed a long hop with another big heave and was bowled.

Concentrate, I told myself again. Mack's dismissal reminded me of something else Kiddo had said, "Watch out for the loose ball," he'd said. "It's the one good batsmen dread. Your concentration lapses, you take a swing and you're out."

Frankie looked hot and sweaty even before he started his innings. But by the time we'd run six singles in the next over he was about to burst. His face was shining like a traffic beacon and he looked like he had been standing under a shower.

"I can't run any more, Hooker," he puffed. "My legs have gone. I'll have to hit a four or I'm dead."

125

He swung a frantic bat at the first two balls of Liam Katz's last over and missed completely. The third was a slow looping off-break and Frankie swung with all his weight. He hit it too early but he got a lot of bat on it and the ball rose high over the bowler's head. Liam turned and ran back for the catch.

"Run!" I yelled to Frankie.

"I can't," he cried. But he set off on the run. Meanwhile Marty was tearing in from long-on and Liam was running towards him watching the ball over his shoulder. I turned for the second run just as they collided.

"Yes," I shouted at Frankie.

"Oh no," he said in despair and lumbered back down the pitch. Marty and Liam were busy untangling themselves, swearing at each other and looking for the ball which was running slowly towards the boundary. I called for the third run as Marty chased after it.

"I'm going to die, I'm going to die," chanted Frankie as he rumbled down the pitch towards me. Marty's throw came in hard and low and it looked as though Frankie would be run out. But he made a last desperate lunge and threw himself over the line. He bounced on his stomach past the stumps and lay gasping and groaning at the umpire's feet.

"Oxygen," moaned Frankie. Steam was rising from his beetroot face and there was a bright green stain the whole length of the front of his shirt and trousers. With a groan he dragged himself to his feet and stood wobbling at the knees as Liam ran in again. We should have got two runs off my next shot, a beautifully placed drive to the right of cover point, but Frankie refused the second run and sat down for another breather. He missed the next ball completely and I went over to talk to him, partly to give him a chance to get his breath back.

"One ball left; make it pay, okay?" I said.

Frankie gasped for air and couldn't reply.

Liam's last ball was well-pitched-up and Frankie stepped

inside it and creamed it hard and high over square-leg for four.

"Only way," he said as he staggered up to me puffing and blowing. "I couldn't run another centimetre."

We'd made 84 and Frankie and I were cheered all the way back to the pavilion.

Cal came out with a bucket of water and two glasses but before I could get a drink Frankie took the bucket and poured the whole lot straight over his head.

HOME TEAM	GLORY GARDENS V WYCKHAM WNDRS	AWAY TEAM	AT EASTGATE PRIORY DATE JUNE 15TH

INNINGS OF GLORY GARDENS.......... TOSS WON BY G.G.... WEATHER SUNNY

BATSMAN	RUNS SCORED	HOW OUT	BOWLER	SCORE
1 M. ROSE	»	bowled	LEAR	0
2 C. SEBASTIEN	2·2·1·2·1·1 »	bowled	MOHAMED	9
3 A. NAZAR	4 »	bowled	LEAR	4
4 E. DAVIES	1·1·1·1·2·1·1·2·1 »	lbw	LEAR	12
5 C. DA COSTA	2·1·1·1·1·4·6 »	st GALE	MOHAMET	17
6 H. KNIGHT	1·2·1·2·3·1·1·1·1·1·1	NOT	OUT	16
7 T. McCURDY	1·4 »	bowled	KATZ	5
8 F. ALLEN	1·1·1·3·4	NOT	OUT	10
9				
10				
11				

FALL OF WICKETS

	1	2	3	4	5	6	7	8	9	10
SCORE	8	12	26	45	57	70				
BAT NO	1	3	2	4	5	7				

BYES	2	2
L.BYES	I	1
WIDES	1·1·2·1·1	6
NO BALLS	N	2

TOTAL EXTRAS	11
TOTAL FOR WKTS	84 / 6

SCORE AT A GLANCE

BOWLING ANALYSIS ⊙ NO BALL + WIDE																
BOWLER	1	2	3	4	5	6	7	8	9	10	11	12	13	OVS	MDS	RUNS	WKT
1 W. REIFER	⊙· 2·	2·	·2·	·+·1	☒									4	0	16	0
2 M. LEAR	M	·w 4w	☒	·6 2·3	☒									4	1	16	3
3 B. WOOLF	·1·1	1·1	1·1	·1·1										4	0	12	0
4 Y. MOHAMED	W	·1 2·1	1·2· 14	2· 1·w	☒									4	1	15	2
5 T. WOOD	1·1 ·1	111												2	0	9	0
6 L. KATZ	·1· 4·N	··3 1·4												2	0	13	1
7																	
8																	
9																	

Chapter Sixteen

The big thing was to get Liam out. He's the best batsman in the Wanderers side by a mile. On his day he's probably the best Under 13s bat in the county – and that includes Azzie; though I'd rather watch Azzie play any day. I'd seen Liam bat plenty of times and he doesn't have any real weaknesses I can spot, except maybe over-confidence. He's especially strong on or outside the leg stump so it's important to bowl an off-stump line to him. If you drift down the leg he'll murder you.

Liam opened the innings with Andy Wood, one of the two Wood brothers in the Wanderers side. I thought I'd give Jacky the end that Marty had bowled from and I'd come on from the Woodcock Lane end. There's not really much of a slope at the Priory but some quick bowlers prefer the canal end because they say there's a bit more bounce in the pitch.

Frankie couldn't find his gloves at the start of the Wanderers innings and he ended up borrowing the opposition's gloves from Charlie Gale.

"I bet Gatting's gone off with them," said Frankie.

"More likely you forgot to put them back in the bag on Saturday," said Cal. Frankie's always losing things because he's so untidy.

Liam began slowly but he never once played and missed. All his defensive shots were right in the middle of the bat. Frankie had a nightmare start. First he dropped Andy Wood off a straightforward chance in Jacky's first over. Then he let two byes through his legs off me.

129

"It's the gloves," he complained. "They're too small for me."

In Jacky's second over Mack picked up a drive left-handed at cover point and threw hard and low, straight over the bails. Frankie dropped it. And Liam Katz escaped being run out for just two runs.

I put my head in my hands. Marty's right, I thought. With Sam behind the stumps we'd have had Liam back in the pavilion and the game in the bag.

Jacky was furious. "If you can't catch the ball with those gloves on, take them off."

"I can't," said Frankie. "I think they're welded on." He was still sweating and puffing in the heat but it didn't stop him talking and joking as usual.

It wasn't long before Liam started to open his shoulders. He hit a cracking cover drive off me and then pulled Jacky fiercely through mid-wicket. The score-board was racing along. Frankie let through two more byes and then he hung on to a diving left-handed catch as Andy Wood snicked my out-swinger.

"I think I'm getting the hang of these gloves," he said. "And that's lucky because I think I'll be wearing them for the rest of my life."

Jacky struck in the next over, clean bowling the new batsman and we'd pegged them back to 26 for two.

In came Charlie Gale. "Let's see the size of your hands," said Frankie. He looked carefully as Charlie took off one of his batting gloves. "Just as I thought," he said. "Minute. Oh well, you'd better get yourself some new gloves because I shall be wearing these all the time from now on."

I bowled my last over at Liam and actually beat him outside the off-stump with a lovely away cutter. But he still scored six off the over. That was the end of my spell and Jacky's, too. He'd taken one for 11, I had one for 16.

Cal and Erica took over the bowling but it was the same story. They both bowled well but Liam latched on to anything loose and whacked it for four. Even I had to admit he was playing beautifully. At the half way stage they were 44 for two and Liam had scored 28 of them.

Erica was in her second over and Liam had just hit her for two twos in succession through the covers. The fifty was on the board already and Wyckham were cruising to an easy win. I was thinking of taking Erica off and bringing on Tylan to vary the attack. She ran in and bowled again – a good ball, on a length just outside off-stump. Liam seemed to hesitate for a split second, then he went through with his stroke. There was a faint but audible click as the ball flicked the bat. Frankie got it in both gloves, fumbled and caught it again between his elbows.

"Owzthat!" he shouted as Mack raced in and grabbed the ball before he could drop it again.

"Th . . . That dog," stuttered Liam, pointing past Erica. We all turned and saw Gatting rolling steadily along in front of the sight-screen. "It put me off," said Liam.

"Sorry about that, old chum," said Frankie. "You can hardly blame us if a dog goes for a walk. You're out."

And Liam walked off, still staring at Gatting who rolled slowly on, unaware of the enormous effect he'd had on the day's events. Liam had scored 32.

"You're beautiful, Gatting," said Frankie. "For that you can keep my gloves."

Getting rid of Liam was a big boost – but it didn't mean we'd won the match, by any means. They still needed only 36 runs with seven wickets remaining and Charlie Gale took over the assault. He took seven runs off Cal's next over including a straight drive back over his head for four. Erica pulled back the balance with a good caught and bowled but I decided it was time for a change of bowling and I brought Tylan on at Cal's end.

It was a strange over. He opened with a wide down the leg side. Then he beat the bat with a fine leg break but it beat Frankie too and they ran two byes. A horrible long hop was pulled for another two followed by an unplayable ball which just missed the stumps. Finally Tylan got one to beat the bat and hit the wicket. 64 for five.

Erica finished an excellent spell with two for 15 and Tylan carried on bowling his allsorts from the bottom end. Another wide, two byes in succession, a full toss – and then he lured Charlie Gale out of his crease and Frankie flicked off the bails with the neatest piece of stumping you could wish to see.

"They're good stumping gloves these," he said to Charlie as Charlie departed. But Frankie didn't know how good!

Win Reifer strolled to the wicket swinging his bat round in big circles. I knew exactly what he'd aim to do and I moved all the leg side fielders out to the boundary. Win launched himself down the wicket at Tylan's first ball and missed with a huge swing. Frankie didn't take it cleanly, but he had time to fumble the ball, control it and knock off the bails before Win got his bat back. Two wickets, two stumpings. Frankie threw the ball in the air and waltzed down the wicket to give Tylan a big high five.

"When did you see Sam Keeping take two stumpings in a row," he said.

"When did you last see him drop a catch, miss a stumping chance and give away a dozen byes," said Cal.

"No one's perfect," grinned Frankie. They were now 72 for seven and with the end of Tylan's over I had a difficult decision to make. There was still Marty to come in and he can score runs if he puts his mind to it. With three overs left to bowl I could bring back Cal for his one remaining over or bowl Mack or Clive. Even though he hasn't played for three weeks I decided on Mack; he's usually reliable in a crisis. Mack measured out his run up while I adjusted the field. Finally he ran in and bowled. The batsman, the second Wood brother, went for a huge drive outside the off-stump. He missed and overbalanced. The ball cannoned into Frankie's pads and bounced back into the stumps.

"Owzthat?" cried a delighted Frankie. The batsman's toe was still over the line and old Sid had no hesitation in giving him out.

"Hat trick!" shouted Mack and Frankie simultaneously.

"Three stumpings in a row," cried Frankie. "Who'd believe it?"

"Outrageous," said Tylan.

"Amazing," said Cal, slapping Frankie on the back. "But you have to ask why the third one left his crease."

"And three wickets in a row for me, too," said Mack.

"You having a brainstorm?" asked Clive.

"No, mate," said Mack. "See, I took two with my last two balls against Arctics – and I haven't bowled since then. So this makes it a hat trick."

"Well, I suppose so," said Clive, not sounding too convinced.

At the end of Mack's over Wyckham had 76. Marty, who was looking very determined, opened his score with a fierce pull past square-leg.

Tylan bowled another wide. A single came off a leg-bye. Marty hit another two – and suddenly they needed only five to win. I could hardly bear it. Surely we weren't going to lose now – not at the hands of Marty!

Tylan bowled again – a loose one down the leg side and Marty swung at it. The ball flew in the air straight as an arrow to square-leg. The fielder didn't have time to think, he just put his hands in front of his face and caught it. It was Ohbert.

"Catch of the season!" shouted Frankie. And it was.

Ohbert just beamed. As Marty passed him on the way back to the pavilion, he said, "Oh but, Marty. Sorry I got you out." That must have pleased Mart.

They still needed five but now the last pair were at the wicket. I knew a lucky boundary would bring the scores level but still I brought the field in to put pressure on the batsmen by cutting out the singles. Tylan bowled the last ball of the

133

Ohbert judges the catch perfectly. He catches it baseball style in front of his face.

over and it cannoned off Bazza Woolf's front pad as he tried to swing it over square-leg. Everyone went up for lbw.

"Not out," said Sid.

I kept the field tight for Mack and the Wyckham players couldn't find a way through it. You could feel the tension mounting. Mack's fourth delivery was on middle stump, the batsman dropped it down in front of him. "Yes," he shouted and set off for a quick single. "No!" screamed Bazza at the other end but it was too late – he had to run. The hesitation was fatal. Mack was on the ball like a terrier. As he picked it up he saw that he could beat Bazza to the stumps. Instead of throwing, he raced in and broke the wicket. Up went Sid's finger at square-leg. We'd won by four runs.

"We've won the League!" screamed Frankie, pulling out a stump and running for the pavilion. Even my sister was cheer-

ing as we came off. Frankie and Cal were carrying a squeal-
ing Ohbert high on their shoulders.

The first person to come and congratulate me was Marty.
"Well played, Hooker," he said. "You deserved it. And I was
wrong – Glory Gardens does play to win."

"Want to play for us again?" I said.

"You bet." His face lit up. "I want to be on the same side
as Ohbert from now on."

Kiddo was out of his mind with excitement. "You've done
yourselves proud, kiddoes. Best team in the county. And four
players in the Colts side."

"What?" said Azzie.

"That's right. Harry, Marty, Asif and Clive have all been
picked to play for the County Colts," said Kiddo.

"Marty doesn't play for us," said Frankie.

"Yes he does," I said.

Frankie got Player of the Match for his hat trick of stumpings and that amazing sweaty innings, and we all decided that
Clive was Player of the Season for his batting, although Cal
had to be close with 10 wickets. You could see Clive thought
we'd made the right decision though.

The only person who didn't look very happy was Liam
Katz. He kept staring at Gatting and scowling. Gatting saw
him and thought he was trying to be friendly. He waddled
over and gave him a big, smelly lick. Even Liam had to laugh
at that.

From the Gazette:
GLORY GARDENS WIN THE LEAGUE
Report by Jo Allen

Glory Gardens won the North & East County Under 13s
League with an exciting victory over their closest challengers,
Wyckham Wanderers, at Eastgate Priory.

Batting first, Glory Gardens put up a tough target of 84
with contributions from Erica Davies (12), Clive da Costa
(17) and Hooker Knight (16 not out). The Wanderers began

well but struggled after their captain, Liam Katz, was out for the top score of 32. The match turned in Glory Gardens' favour when three wickets fell in three balls with the score on 72. All three batsmen were stumped by wicket-keeper, Francis Allen – is this a record? Tylan Vellacott took four wickets for 9 runs and Erica Davies two for 15. Wyckham were all out in the final over for 80.

Francis Allen was awarded Player of the Match and Clive da Costa voted Player of the Season.

"I bet she hated writing all those nice things about me," said Frankie.

HOME TEAM	GLORY GARDENS	V	WYCKHAM WNDRS	AWAY TEAM	AT EASTGATE PRIORY. DATE JUNE 15TH

INNINGS OF WYCKHAM WANDERERS .... TOSS WON BY G.G. WEATHER SUNNY.

BATSMAN	RUNS SCORED	HOW OUT	BOWLER	SCORE
1 L.KATZ	1·1·1·2·4·1·4·2·2·2·4·4·2·2 >>	ct ALLEN	DAVIES	32
2 A.WOOD	1·1·1 >>	ct ALLEN	KNIGHT	4
3 B.TATE	1·2 >>	bowled	GUNN	3
4 C.GALE	1·2·2·2·4·1·2·1·2 >>	st ALLEN	VELLACOTT	17
5 D.O'LEARY	2 >>	c & b	DAVIES	2
6 Y.MOHAMED	2 >>	bowled	VELLACOTT	2
7 T.WOOD	>>	st ALLEN	McCURDY	0
8 W.REIFER	>>	st ALLEN	VELLACOTT	0
9 M.LEAR	2·2 >>	ct BENNETT	VELLACOTT	4
10 J.BUTT	1·	NOT	OUT	1·
11 B.WOOLF	>>	RUN	OUT	0

FALL OF WICKETS											BYES	2·1·1·1·2·1·1		9	TOTAL EXTRAS	15
SCORE	23	26	50	59	64	72	72	72	80	80	LBYES	1·1·		2	TOTAL FOR	80
	1	2	3	4	5	6	7	8	9	10	WIDES	1·1·1		3		
BAT NO	2	3	1	5	6	4	8	7	9	11	NO BALLS	1·		1	WKTS	10

SCORE AT A GLANCE

BOWLER	BOWLING ANALYSIS ⊙ NO BALL + WIDE													OVS	MDS	RUNS	WKT
	1	2	3	4	5	6	7	8	9	10	11	12	13				
1 J.GUNN	1··	·:·12	··4·W··	·2·V··	X									4	0	11	1
2 H.KNIGHT	1··	··4	W··12	2·2·	X									4	0	16	1
3 C.SEBASTIEN	··4·	2···	·2·4·1		X									3	0	14	0
4 E.DAVIES	··2·4	·22 W··	··2·W··	··2·1	X									4	0	15	2
5 T.VELLACOTT	+·· 2·W	+·+· RWW	+·+· 2V·											3	0	9	4
6 T.McCURDY	W0··3	···												1·4	0	4	1
7																	
8																	
9																	

FINAL LEAGUE POSITIONS

	PLAYED	WON	LOST	TIED	PTS
Glory Gardens	6	5	0	1	57*
Wyckham Wanderers	7	5	2	0	50
Old Courtiers	6	4	1	1	47*
Croyland Crusaders	7	4	3	0	40
Stoneyheath	7	3	4	0	30
Arctics	6	2	4	0	22*
Brass Castle	6	1	5	0	12*
Waterville	7	1	6	0	10

*2 points for cancelled match

Final Round Results:
Glory Gardens *beat* **Wyckham Wanderers by 4 runs**
Old Courtiers *beat* **Stoneyheath & Stockton by 3 wickets**
Brass Castle *lost to* **Waterville by 21 runs**
Arctics *beat* **Croyland Crusaders by 9 runs**

AVERAGE

Batting

	INN	N/O	RUNS	S/R	H/S	AVERAGE
Clive	5	0	88	90.7	46	17.6
Hooker	5	2	65	86.7	20	21.7
Azzie	6	0	64	91.4	24	10.7
Matthew	6	0	39	29.8	15	6.5
Erica	6	2	37	50.7	15*	9.3
Cal	6	0	36	35.3	14	6.0

*signifies 'not out'. Scoring Rate (S/R) is based on the average number of runs scored per 100 balls. H/S = highest score. Minimum qualification. 30 runs.

Bowling

	OVERS	RUNS	WKTS	S/R	ECON	BB	AVERAGE
Cal	22.4	72	10	13.6	3.2	3/5	7.2
Jacky	23	58	9	15.3	2.5	2/4	6.4
Hooker	15	49	8	11.3	3.3	3/11	6.1
Erica	17	43	7	14.6	2.5	2/5	6.1
Tylan	13	54	6	13.0	4.2	4/9	9.0
Marty	12	38	3	24.0	3.2	2/9	12.7

Strike Rate (S/R) shows that Cal takes a wicket every 13.6 balls. Economy Rates (ECON) is the average number of runs given away each over. BB = Best bowling performance.

Breakdown of bowling performances

	WKTS	BOWLED	CAUGHT	LBW	STUMPED	HT WKT
Cal	10	2	6	-	1	1
Jacky	9	3	4	-	2	-
Hooker	8	3	5	-	-	-
Erica	7	2	3	2	-	-
Tylan	6	1	3	-	2	-
Marty	3	2	-	1	-	-

Minimum qualification: 10 overs

Catching

	CAUGHT	DROPPED	AGGREGATE
Sam	5	-	+5
Frankie	6	4	+2
Mack	3	1	+2
Cal	2	-	+2
Erica	2	-	+2
Tylan	1	-	+1
Clive	1	-	+1
Azzie	1	1	0
Ohbert	1	2	-1
Marty	0	1	-1
Matthew	0	2	-2
Hooker	1	4	-3

Wicket-keeping

	TOTAL	STUMPED	CAUGHT
Frankie	8	4	4
Sam	7	2	5

Jo Allen's League Ratings

Players are rated over the season. Bowlers' and batsmens' ratings are worked out match by match against the team's average performance. Extra points are added for batting scores over 20, 30, etc and wickets taken in a match over 3, 4, etc.

BOWLING		Pts	BATTING		Pts
C. Sebastien	GG	837	L. Katz	WW	850
J. Bennetto	OC	793	C. da Costa	GG	815
Y. Mohamed	WW	770	R. Mattis	OC	775
S. McLachlan	A	705	F. Duffield	CC	721
J. Gunn	GG	698	H. Knight	GG	640
H. Knight	GG	673	O. Sheringham	S&S	635

THE CRICKET PITCH

crease   At each end of the wicket the crease is marked out in white paint like this:

Return crease

Popping or batting crease

Stumps

The batsman is 'in his ground' when his bat or either foot are behind the batting or 'popping' crease. He can only be given out 'stumped' or 'run out' if he is outside the crease.

The bowler must not put his front foot down beyond the popping crease when he bowls. And his back foot must be inside the return crease. If he breaks these rules the umpire will call a 'no ball'.

leg side/   The cricket pitch is divided down the middle.
off-side   Everything on the side of the batsman's legs is called the 'leg side' or 'on side' and the other side is called the 'off-side'.

Remember, when a left-handed bat is batting, his legs are on the other side. So leg side and off-side switch round.

leg stump   Three stumps and two bails make up each wicket. The 'leg stump' is on the same side as the batsman's legs. Next to it is the 'middle stump' and then the 'off-stump'.

141

off/on side	See **leg side**
off-stump	See **leg stump**
pitch	The 'pitch' is the area between the two wickets. It is 22 yards long from wicket to wicket (although it's usually 20 yards for Under 11s and 21 yards for Under 13s). The grass on the pitch is closely mown and rolled flat. Just to make things confusing, sometimes the whole ground is called a 'cricket pitch'.
square	The area in the centre of the ground where the strips are.
strip	Another name for the pitch. They are called strips because there are several pitches side by side on the square. A different one is used for each match.
track	Another name for the pitch or strip.
wicket	'Wicket' means two things, so it can sometimes confuse people. 1 The stumps and bails at each end of the pitch. The batsman defends his wicket. 2 The pitch itself. So you can talk about a hard wicket or a turning wicket (if it's taking spin).

BATTING

attacking strokes	The attacking strokes in cricket all have names. There are forward strokes (played off the front foot) and backward strokes (played

142

off the back foot). The drawing shows where the different strokes are played around the wicket.

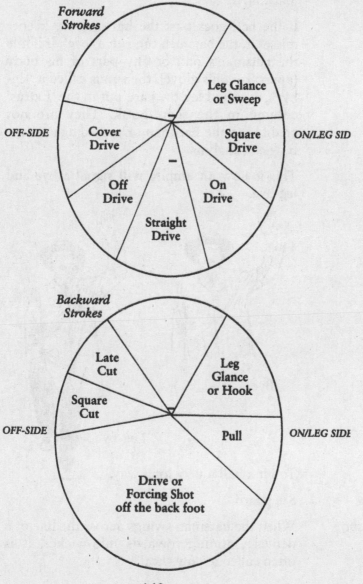

Forward Strokes

Leg Glance or Sweep

OFF-SIDE

Cover Drive

Square Drive

ON/LEG SID

Off Drive

On Drive

Straight Drive

Backward Strokes

Late Cut

Leg Glance or Hook

Square Cut

OFF-SIDE

Pull

ON/LEG SIDE

Drive or Forcing Shot off the back foot

backing up	As the bowler bowls, the non-striking batsman should start moving down the wicket to be ready to run a quick single. This is called 'backing up'.
bye	If the ball goes past the bat and the keeper misses it, the batsmen can run a 'bye'. If it hits the batsman's pad or any part of his body (apart from his glove), the run is called a 'leg-bye'. Byes and leg-byes are put in the 'Extras' column in the score-book. They are not credited to the batsman or scored against the bowler's analysis.
	This is how an umpire will signal a bye and leg-bye.

Bye

Leg-bye

cart	To hit a ball a very long way.
centre	See **guard**
cow shot	When the batsman swings across the line of a delivery, aiming towards mid-wicket, it is often called a 'cow shot'.

144

defensive strokes	There are basically two defensive shots: the 'forward defensive', played off the front foot and the 'backward defensive' played off the back foot.
duck	When a batsman is out before scoring any runs it's called a 'duck'. If he's out first ball for nought it's a 'golden duck'.
gate	If a batsman is bowled after the ball has passed between his bat and pads it is sometimes described as being bowled 'through the gate'.
guard	When you go in to bat the first thing you do is 'take your guard'. You hold your bat sideways in front of the stumps and ask the umpire to give you a guard. He'll show you which way to move the bat until it's in the right position. The usual guards are 'leg stump' (sometimes called 'one leg'); 'middle and leg' ('two leg') and 'centre' or 'middle'.

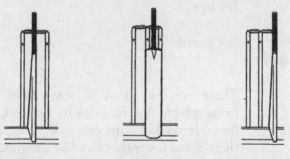

Centre   Middle and leg   Leg

hit wicket	If the batsman knocks off a bail with his bat

145

or any part of his body when the ball is in play, he is out 'hit wicket'.

innings
This means a batsman's stay at the wicket. 'It was the best *innings* I'd seen Azzie play.'
But it can also mean the batting score of the whole team. 'In their first *innings* England scored 360.'

knock
Another word for a batsman's innings.

lbw
Means leg before wicket. In fact a batsman can be given out lbw if the ball hits any part of his body and the umpire thinks it would have hit the stumps. There are two important extra things to remember about lbw:
1 If the ball pitches outside the leg stump and hits the batsman's pads it's not out – even if the ball would have hit the stumps.
2 If the ball pitches outside the off-stump and hits the pad outside the line, it's not out if the batsman is playing a shot. If he's not playing a shot he can still be given out.

leg-bye
See bye

middle/
middle and leg
See guard

out
There are six common ways of a batsman being given out in cricket: bowled, caught, lbw, hit wicket, run out and stumped. Then there are a few rare ones like handled the ball and hit the ball twice. When the fielding side thinks the batsman is out they must appeal (usually a shout of 'Owzthat'). If the umpire

146

considers the batsman is out, he will signal 'out' like this:

play forward/back	You play forward by moving your front foot down the wicket towards the bowler as you play the ball. You play back by putting your weight on the back foot and leaning towards the stumps. You play forward to well-pitched-up bowling and back to short-pitched bowling.
rabbit	Poor or tail-end batsman.
run	A run is scored when the batsman hits the ball and runs the length of the pitch. If he fails to reach the popping crease before the ball is thrown in and the bails are taken off, he is 'run out'. Four runs are scored when the ball is hit across the boundary. Six runs are scored when it crosses the boundary without bouncing. This is how the umpire signals 'four':

This is how the umpire signals 'six':

If the batsman does not put his bat down inside the popping crease at the end of a run before setting off on another run, the umpire will signal 'one short' like this.

A run is then deducted from the total by the scorer.

stance

The stance is the way a batsman stands and holds his bat when he is waiting to receive a delivery. There are many different types of stance. For instance, 'side on', with the shoulder pointing down the wicket; 'square on', with the body turned towards the bowler; 'bat raised' and so on.

striker	The batsman who is receiving the bowling. The batsman at the other end is called the non-striker.
stumped	If you play and miss and the wicket-keeper knocks a bail off with the ball in his hands, you will be out 'stumped' if you are out of your crease.
ton	A century. One hundred runs scored by a batsman.

BOWLING

arm ball	A variation by the off-spinner (or left-arm spinner) which swings in the air in the opposite direction to the normal spin, i.e. away from the right-handed batsman in the case of the off-spinner.
beamer	See **full toss.**
block hole	A ball bowled at yorker length is said to pitch in the 'block hole' – i.e. the place where the batsman marks his guard and rests his bat on the ground when receiving.
bouncer	The bowler pitches the ball very short and bowls it hard into the ground to get extra bounce and surprise the batsman. The ball will often reach the batsman at shoulder height or above. But you have to be a fast bowler to bowl a good bouncer. A slow bouncer is often called a 'long hop' and is easy to pull or cut for four.

chinaman   A left-arm bowler who bowls with the normal leg-break action will deliver an off-break to the right-handed batsman. This is called a 'chinaman'.

dot ball   A ball from which the batsman does not score a run. It is called this because it goes down as a dot in the score-book.

flipper   A variation on the leg-break. It is bowled from beneath the wrist, squeezed out of the fingers, and it skids off the pitch and goes straight through. It shouldn't be attempted by young cricketers because it puts a lot of strain on the wrist and arm ligaments.

full toss   A ball which doesn't bounce before reaching the batsman is a full toss. Normally it's easy to score off a full toss, so it's considered a bad ball. A high full toss from a fast bowler is called a 'beamer'. It is very dangerous and should never be bowled deliberately.

googly   A 'googly' is an off-break bowled with a leg break action (see **leg break**) out of the back of the hand like this.

grubber	A ball which hardly bounces – it pitches and shoots through very low, usually after hitting a bump or crack in the pitch. Sometimes also called a shooter.
hat trick	Three wickets from three consecutive balls by one bowler. They don't have to be in the same over i.e. two wickets from the last two balls of one over and one from the first of the next.
half-volley	See **length**
leg break/ off-break	The 'leg break' is a delivery from a spinner which turns from leg to off. An 'off-break' turns from off to leg. That's easy to remember when it's a right-hand bowler bowling to a right-hand batsman. But when a right-arm, off-break bowler bowls to a left-handed bat he is bowling leg-breaks. And a left-hander bowling with an off-break action bowls leg-breaks to a right-hander. It takes some working out – but the drawing helps.

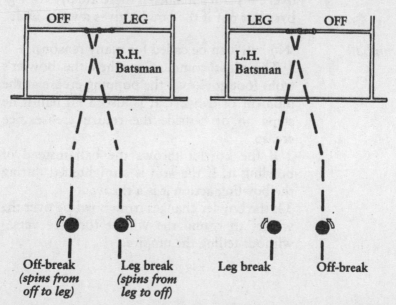

leg-cutter/ *off-cutter*	A ball which cuts away off the pitch from leg to off is a 'leg-cutter'. The 'off-cutter' goes from off to leg. Both these deliveries are bowled by fast or medium-pace bowlers. See **seam bowling**.
leggie	Slang for a leg-spin bowler.
length	You talk about the 'length' or 'pitch' of a ball bowled. A good length ball is one that makes the batsman unsure whether to play back or forward. A short-of-a-length ball pitches slightly closer to the bowler than a good length. A very short-pitched ball is called a 'long hop'. A 'half-volley' is an over-pitched ball which bounces just in front of the batsman and is easy to drive.
long hop	A ball which pitches very short. See **length**.
maiden over	If a bowler bowls an over without a single run being scored off the bat, it's called a 'maiden over'. It's still a maiden if there are byes or leg-byes but not if the bowler gives away a wide.
no ball	'No ball' can be called for many reasons. 1 The most common is when the bowler's front foot goes over the popping crease at the moment of delivery. It is also a no ball if he steps on or outside the return crease. See **crease**. 2 If the bowler throws the ball instead of bowling it. If the arm is straightened during the bowling action it is a throw. 3 If the bowler changes from bowling over the wicket to round the wicket (or vice versa) without telling the umpire.

4 If there are more than two fielders behind square on the leg side. (There are other fielding regulations with the limited overs game. For instance, the number of players who have to be within the circle.)

A batsman can't be out off a no ball, except run out. A penalty of one run (an experiment of two runs is being tried in county cricket) is added to the score and an extra ball must be bowled in the over. The umpire shouts 'no ball' and signals like this:

over the wicket

If a right-arm bowler delivers the ball from the right of the stumps (as seen by the batsman) i.e. with his bowling arm closest to the stumps, then he is bowling 'over the wicket'. If he bowls from the other side of the stumps he is bowling 'round the wicket'.

pace

The pace of the ball is the speed it is bowled at. A fast or pace bowler like Waqar Younis can bowl at speeds of up to 90 miles an hour. The different speeds of bowlers range from fast through medium to slow with in-between speeds like fast-medium and medium-fast (fast-medium is the faster).

pitch	See length.
round the wicket	See over the wicket
seam	The seam is the sewn, raised ridge which runs round a cricket ball.
seam bowling	Bowling – usually medium to fast – where the ball cuts into or away from the batsman off the seam.
shooter	See *grubber*.
spell	A 'spell' of bowling is the number of overs bowled in succession by a bowler. So if a bowler bowls six overs before being replaced by another bowler, he has bowled a spell of six overs.
swing bowling	A cricket ball can be bowled to swing through the air. It has to be bowled in a particular way to achieve this and one side of the ball must be polished and shiny. Which is why you always see fast bowlers shining the ball. An 'in-swinger' swings into the batsman's legs from the off-side. An 'out-swinger' swings away towards the slips.
trundler	A steady, medium-pace bowler who is not particularly good.
turn	Another word for spin. You can say 'the ball turned a long way' or 'it spun a long way'.
wicket maiden	An over when no run is scored off the bat and the bowler takes one wicket or more.

wide	If the ball is bowled too far down the leg side or the off-side for the batsman to reach (usually the edge of the return crease is the line umpires look for) it is called a 'wide'. One run is added to the score and an extra ball is bowled in the over. In limited overs cricket wides are given for balls closer to the stumps – any ball bowled down the leg side risks being called a wide in this sort of 'one-day' cricket. This is how an umpire signals a wide.

yorker	A ball, usually a fast one – bowled to bounce precisely under the batsman's bat. The most dangerous yorker is fired in fast towards the batsman's legs to hit leg stump.

FIELDING

backing up	A fielder backs up a throw to the wicket-keeper or bowler by making sure it doesn't go for overthrows. So when a throw comes in to the keeper, a fielder is positioned behind him to cover him if he misses it. Not to be confused with a *batsman* backing up.
chance	A catchable ball. So to miss a chance is the same as to drop a catch.

close/deep	Fielders are either placed close to the wicket (near the batsman) or in the deep or 'out-field' (near the boundary).
cow corner	The area between the deep mid-wicket and long-on boundaries where a *cow shot* is hit to.
dolly	An easy catch.
hole-out	A slang expression for a batsman being caught. 'He holed out at mid-on.'
overthrow	If the ball is thrown to the keeper or the bowler's end and is misfielded allowing the batsmen to take extra runs, these are called 'overthrows'.
silly	A fielding position very close to the batsman and in front of the wicket e.g. silly mid-on.
sledging	Using abusive language and swearing at a batsman to put him off. A slang expression – first used in Australia.
square	Fielders 'square' of the wicket are on a line with the batsman on either side of the wicket. If they are fielding further back from this line, they are 'behind square' or 'backward of square'; if they are fielding in front of the line i.e. closer to the bowler, they are 'in front of square' or 'forward of square'.
standing up/ standing back	The wicket-keeper 'stands up' to the stumps for slow bowlers. This means he takes his

position immediately behind the stumps. For fast bowlers he stands well back – often several yards away for very quick bowlers. He may either stand up or back for medium-pace bowlers.

GENERAL WORDS

colts

County Colts teams are selected from the best young cricketers in the county at all ages from Under 11 to Under 17. Junior league cricket is usually run by the County Colts Association.

under 11s/ 12s etc.

You qualify for an Under 11 team if you are 11 or under on September 1st prior to the cricket season. So if you're 12 but you were 11 on September 1st last year, you can play for the Under 11s.

———————— ● ————————

FIELDING POSITIONS

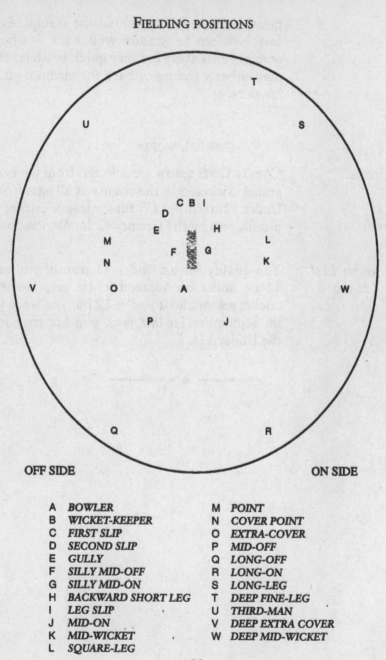

OFF SIDE   ON SIDE

A	*BOWLER*	M	*POINT*
B	*WICKET-KEEPER*	N	*COVER POINT*
C	*FIRST SLIP*	O	*EXTRA-COVER*
D	*SECOND SLIP*	P	*MID-OFF*
E	*GULLY*	Q	*LONG-OFF*
F	*SILLY MID-OFF*	R	*LONG-ON*
G	*SILLY MID-ON*	S	*LONG-LEG*
H	*BACKWARD SHORT LEG*	T	*DEEP FINE-LEG*
I	*LEG SLIP*	U	*THIRD-MAN*
J	*MID-ON*	V	*DEEP EXTRA COVER*
K	*MID-WICKET*	W	*DEEP MID-WICKET*
L	*SQUARE-LEG*		

GLORY
GARDENS
CRICKET CLUB

GLORY IN
THE CUP

BOB CATTELL

Hooker, Azzie, Erica and the rest all play cricket in their spare time, but they've never taken it very seriously until now. Kiddo, one of their school teachers, suggests they form an official team and play proper matches – and Glory Gardens C.C. is formed. Hooker, as captain, soon finds out that cricket teams weren't built in a day: some players squabble, some can't catch, and some have tantrums and go home at half-time! So will Glory Gardens go all out for victory . . . or will they be out for a duck?

ISBN – 978 0 099 46111 1
RED FOX
£4.99

GLORY
GARDENS
CRICKET CLUB

BOUND
FOR GLORY

BOB CATTELL

Glory Gardens C.C. is now in the North County
Under Thirteen League, and the pressure is really on.
Hooker, as captain, worries that the team won't be able
to hold it together: arrogant Clive is always picking fights,
Ohbert is still as useless as ever, and there are all the usual
rows and injuries. But there's also Mack, the new player;
the lucky mascot, 'Gatting'; plus the whole team's
unwavering determination to win against
all the odds.

ISBN – 978 0 099 46121 0
RED FOX
£4.99